Quinn Sat Quietly, Watching The Sleeping Woman.

Jennifer had amazed him these past two days with her stoicism. He had seen her exhausted. He had seen her in pain. He had seen her sweltering in the heat. She had never shown her fear. Perhaps she didn't have sense enough to be afraid. Perhaps she didn't understand the constant perils that accompanied their flight.

They could be stopped at any time. They could be taken into custody by a government not known for its humane practices.

At the very least she should be afraid of him—shouldn't she? And yet whenever she looked at him her gaze was clear and steady.

He'd never met another woman like her, and he found himself unwillingly admiring her.

Quinn had met very few women he admired.

Dear Reader:

I hope you've been enjoying 1989, our "Year of the Man" at Silhouette Desire. Every one of the twelve authors who are contributing a *Man of the Month* has created a very special someone for your reading pleasure. Each man is unique, and each author's style and characterization give you a different insight into her man's story.

From January to December, 1989 will be a twelve-month extravaganza spotlighting one book each month with special cover treatment as a tribute to the Silhouette Desire hero—our *Man of the Month*!

Created by your favorite authors, these men are utterly captivating—and I think Mr. June, Annette Broadrick's Quinn McNamara, will be simply...*Irresistible*! One of Lass Small's Lambert sisters gets a very special man in July. *Man of the Month* Graham Rawlins may start as the *Odd Man Out*, but that doesn't last long....

Yours,

Isabel Swift

Senior Editor & Editorial Coordinator

ANNETTE BROADRICK
Irresistible

Silhouette Desire

Published by Silhouette Books New York

America's Publisher of Contemporary Romance

SILHOUETTE BOOKS
300 East 42nd St., New York, N.Y. 10017

ISBN: 0-373-05499-8

First Silhouette Books printing June 1989

Books by Annette Broadrick

Silhouette Desire

Hunter's Prey #185
Bachelor Father #219
Hawk's Flight #242
Deceptions #272
Choices #283
Heat of the Night #314
Made in Heaven #336
Return to Yesterday #360
Adam's Story #367
Momentary Marriage #414
With All My Heart #433
A Touch of Spring #464
Irresistible #499

Silhouette Romance

Circumstantial Evidence #329
Provocative Peril #359
Sound of Summer #412
Unheavenly Angel #442
Strange Enchantment #501
Mystery Lover #533
That's What Friends Are For #544
Come Be My Love #609

Silhouette Christmas Stories 1988

"Christmas Magic"

ANNETTE BROADRICK

lives on the shores of the Lake of the Ozarks in Missouri, where she spends her time doing what she loves most—reading and writing romantic fiction. "For twenty-five years I lived in various large cities, working as a legal secretary, a very high-stress occupation. I never thought I was capable of making a career change at this point in my life, but thanks to Silhouette I am now able to write full-time in the peaceful surroundings that have turned my life into a dream come true."

This book is dedicated to
Denise Crundall of Melbourne
and her continuing crusade for
peace and harmony on the planet.

One

Quinn glanced at his wristwatch, took one last draw on his cigarette and dropped the remainder of the burning cylinder to the ground. After crushing all sparks with the heel of his combat boot, he carefully fieldstripped what remained, out of habit more than any desire to conceal his position there on the edge of the small North African settlement. One more Turkish cigarette butt in the area wouldn't draw any undue attention.

Such habits were a way of life to him by now. Quinn had managed to stay alive for the past eighteen months by leaving nothing to chance. He made very few mistakes because he thought through every move he planned to make. Staying alive was a conscious decision on his part, made daily.

Glancing around the dry rocky area, he began to make his way along the ravine that separated the village from the surrounding desert. He gave little thought to the hours he had just spent observing what was taking place in the village, because that was his job—gathering information. Patience had become an integral part of his nature over the years.

Quinn felt a trickle of perspiration slide along his cheekbone. Absently he took the end of the kerchief tied around his throat and wiped his face, then pulled his cap low to shade his eyes from the setting sun. Squinting beneath the brim of his hat, he glanced around the dusty village as he continued along the side of the ravine.

He certainly hadn't come to this godforsaken place for a vacation or because of his health. An unfortunate aspect of his line of work included being sent to the less glamorous parts of the world.

Maybe he'd hit Max up for a raise, he thought with a slight smile. A request for a transfer would be out of the question. He'd spent eighteen months living with the local inhabitants of Shiran, listening—always listening—and watching, gathering as much information as he could.

Shiran was the most recent name given to this small desert country, whose strategic location and oil reserves drew a great deal of interest from other countries, the United States included.

Max had warned him that this assignment would be tough. He had also made it clear that Quinn was uniquely suited for the job, both because of his looks and his background.

So far, so good. He had managed to gain the trust of a group of men who were working to oust the present government. At long last he had been invited to sit in on their meetings, to hear the plans, to get some idea of what was happening in the rebel camp.

The meeting tonight was important, one he hoped would produce information that would fill some of the gaps in what he'd managed to gather.

What he had to discover tonight was what position the rebels would take toward the United States government if they were successful with their coup. He needed to find out who in the rebel organization favored cooperation with the United States, who wanted closer ties to the Soviet Union, and who wanted alliance with one or more of the Islamic groups operating in North Africa and the Middle East.

He paused, listening to the sounds that accompanied the approaching night. There were no unidentifiable noises. He turned down a narrow alleyway that led to the meeting place, moving silently in the shaded space. He was early. He knew that. He hoped to have a chance to speak with Omar, the leader.

The small shop that Quinn stepped into was hot and dusty. Nodding without speaking to the shopkeeper, he went behind a curtain and down a long hallway. He stopped at the first door, tapped a prearranged signal and waited.

When the door opened, Quinn stepped into the meeting room and became Rashid Quoram, playing a role that had become second nature to him.

"You're early," Hamid pointed out brusquely in Arabic.

"Yes," Quinn agreed in the same language, his gaze immediately going to a corner of the small room where three men were gathered, looking at something that remained blocked from Quinn's view. "What's going on?"

Hamid shrugged and walked over to the group. Quinn followed, curious at the degree of tension in the room. He moved closer. Then he saw what was causing it.

There was a woman tied to the chair she was sitting in—a woman with long blond hair that at one time had been in a braid but was now knotted and gnarled. One cheek was scraped and bruised.

She sat there with her head down, as though ignoring the men who stood around her.

He leaned against the wall, fighting to maintain his air of detachment despite what he saw. "Who is she?"

His question caused an immediate halt in the conversation. Omar turned away from the discussion he'd been having with the other two men and walked over to where Quinn stood.

"Ah, Rashid," he said with a genial smile. "You're early. You must be eager to begin."

Quinn nodded his head toward the woman. "Have we declared war on women now, Omar? What's going on?"

Omar smiled. "No, my friend. I'm afraid it's a matter of overzealousness on the part of the men. They had an opportunity to take this woman this afternoon, so they decided she might be of value to us in promoting our cause."

"In what way?"

"They thought perhaps to call attention to our little group with some publicity. An American hostage is still news in this part of the world. However, I've explained to them their error. Now we must decide what to do with the lady." He leaned his shoulder against the wall, imitating Quinn's position, and cocked his head.

"What would you suggest we do with her, Rashid? She's no good to us here and will cause a great deal of harm to our cause if she is found with us."

An American woman! What the hell was she doing in Shiran? Where did she think this was, Disneyland?

"Let her go, perhaps?" he asked dryly.

Omar shook his head. "That was my first thought, too, my friend, but I'm afraid that will not serve. She has already seen too many of us. As I have explained in recent weeks, our advantage has been secrecy. We don't want anyone to know of our existence until we make our move." He motioned to the two men behind him. "Unfortunately, they were hoping for a little personal glory, I'm afraid. In essence, I have two problems here that I must resolve."

From the expression on Omar's face, Quinn seriously doubted that the two men would survive the resolution. What Omar decided to do about the men

was of no concern to him at the moment. What he had
to deal with was the American woman who was creating a most delicate situation for him.

"An American, is she?" he asked, trying to give
himself some time to decide what he could do about
her. "Why is she here in Shiran?"

"She's working with some do-gooder's group,
feeding the hungry, that sort of thing."

"Why the hell did your men decide to take her?"

Omar shrugged. "Because she was there. She was
traveling with two men. I'm afraid both men were shot
in the struggle to escape. The woman tried to run, but
they stopped her." He glanced around at her once
more, and Quinn's gaze followed.

She had raised her head now and was looking at
Quinn. For a moment their gazes clashed. Her eyes
were a clear blue and they stared at him with con-
tempt.

Stupid woman. Doesn't she have any idea of the
danger she's in? he thought with disgust. It would
serve her right if he stayed out of it and let them kill
her. He was sure that was what Omar had in mind. A
disappearing tourist was less of an embarrassment
than one held hostage.

Quinn knew that he couldn't allow his temper to
surface. However, he had a strong urge to hit something. Damn. Why did something like this have to
come up now of all times? He knew as well as Omar
did that publicly acknowledging that they had taken a
hostage would be suicide for their small group. Letting her go to complain about her harsh treatment

would be just as detrimental. That didn't leave too many choices.

Quinn forced himself to shrug, knowing that Omar was watching him closely to see how squeamish he would be about getting rid of the woman. Quinn knew he was still being tested, not for his belief in the cause, because he'd been convincing enough, but for his cold-bloodedness regarding anything that might hamper their cause.

"Do you have any suggestions?" Omar asked after a moment.

"About what?"

"How we should rid ourselves of the lady."

Quinn's mind had gone into overdrive. They were going to kill her unless he could do something—any-thing—to prevent it. And he would have to attempt to save her without blowing his cover! He glanced around the room and realized that while he and Omar had been talking, several more had joined them.

"Life is rough in our country. Many people have disappeared traveling through the remote regions, never to be heard of again." His tone was casual. "Would you like me to take care of the matter?"

Omar glanced at the woman. "She would not last long out in the desert, not with that fair skin."

"No," Quinn agreed, following his gaze. "She wouldn't."

Omar nodded to the two men who stood near her. "Take her into the other room and keep her there un-til after the meeting." He glanced at his watch. "It's time to begin."

Quinn watched the men untie her and pull her to her feet. If looks could kill, they would have withered in their tracks. She jerked her arms away from them and started to take a step, only to cry out and stumble. If one of them hadn't caught her, she would have fallen.

Quinn glanced down and saw that her leg was bleeding and one ankle was swollen. The men glanced at Omar, and he motioned for them to pick her up. One of them bent over and pulled her onto his shoulder in the fireman's hold and started toward the door.

As they moved past him, she raised her head and glared at him. What the hell? Did she think all of this was his fault? He hadn't been the one playing tourist in a strife-filled country, for God's sake.

He impassively watched as the men disappeared through the doorway, but his brain was racing with ideas as to what to do with her.

For the next forty-five minutes, Quinn forced himself to concentrate on what was being discussed. This group had an excellent system of infiltration into the present government. They had people in each department, knew each strong point. More importantly, they knew the weakest links in the chain of command. They were leaving nothing to chance.

Quinn could objectively admire their talent. They were good. Some of them had been trained in the Soviet Union, some in the United States, and others in various parts of the Middle East. Their group was small, but they were not amateurs.

He waited until the rest of the men left before approaching Omar. "Do you want me to get rid of the woman?'' he asked, inclining his head toward the hallway.

Omar shrugged. "If you wish. What do you intend to do with her?''

Good question. If only he knew.

''I'll think of something. The most important thing is to get her out of the village before someone sees her.''

Omar nodded. "Do you need any help?''

Quinn allowed himself a rather feral grin. "I'd prefer to handle this one alone.''

Omar smiled. "Ah, yes, I'm sure you would. Too bad I don't have time for a little sport with her, myself. But we've got too much to do.''

Quinn nodded. What the hell was he going to do with her? he wondered. He'd just bought her some time, but not much. He'd have to talk to her, find out if she knew anyone who could help her. He knew he was compromising his position, particularly if she was discovered later, but damn it, he had no choice.

Quinn wished to hell Washington would stop these people from coming to strife-filled countries. They were asking for whatever happened to them. They didn't care what their families were going through back home, they didn't care what embarrassing situations they caused their government. They were determined to ignore the dangers, just as this woman had done.

He wondered how many other Americans had disappeared over here, never to be heard from again. He shook his head and started down the hallway.

When he opened the door, the two men straightened, coming to attention. He ignored them and walked over to the woman. Once again they had tied her hands to the chair. With her ankle as it was, he could see why they weren't afraid she'd try to escape. She couldn't even walk.

He spoke to the men in Arabic, explaining that they could go and that he would deal with the situation. They both looked relieved and headed out of the room. No doubt Omar would be waiting for them.

However, that wasn't his problem at the moment. She watched him come closer, her gaze never leaving his. He could see the apprehension but was too angry to reassure her. Let her think he was one of her captors. She could so easily compromise his position there.

One thing for sure, he had to get her away from there. Maybe he could take her north, toward the capital city of Sirocco on the coast. The desert lay in between. If he could convince Omar that he intended to take her out to the desert and leave her, he would gain a few days before Omar would become suspicious about his failure to return.

He realized that he might not be able to come back. By helping this woman, he would have to tell her who he was. Otherwise he knew she would not cooperate. And he didn't want to harm her. Not really. Although at the moment his anger was such that he could have throttled her with little provocation.

He untied her, then picked her up in his arms rather than placing her across his shoulder. She looked at him, startled, then hesitantly placed her arms around his neck, clasping them behind him. She was small, he noticed, more aware of her than he wished to be.

He carried her down the hallway, heading toward the door that led to the street where Omar's Jeep would be parked. He would have to go back to his room and get his things. He calculated the risks involved and the preparations needed.

She rested her head on his shoulder and he glanced down at her. The only color in her face came from the angry bruises on her cheek. Otherwise she was white.

As soon as he reached the street, he found Omar waiting for him. "My Jeep is parked over there." He pointed to it.

"Yes," Quinn replied. He glanced down to find that the woman had closed her eyes. He carried her to the Jeep and placed her in the passenger's seat. Omar followed him.

"I realize this is not your problem—" Omar began to say when Quinn interrupted.

"She is a danger to our mission. I'll dispose of her, you may be sure of that."

"Get back as soon as you can," the other man said, turning away.

"What are you going to do with me?" she whispered, pulling away from his hands and staring up at him. She surprised him by speaking Arabic. He hadn't expected that. Did she understand it, as well? If so, then she had understood what he had just said to Omar.

He refused to meet her gaze. Instead he walked around the Jeep and crawled into the driver's seat. He started the engine and turned on the lights. Few people were stirring on the street after dark. He shifted gears and pulled away from the curb, headed for his lodgings.

No one was around when he entered the small house where he rented a room. He placed her on his bed and went to get a basin of water and first aid supplies. When he returned with them, he knelt beside the bed and bathed her cheek and leg. The injury to her leg was slight except for the ankle. She'd probably turned it when she'd tried to run away.

He glanced up when he was through and caught her watching him, her eyes shadowed. He could feel her tension, see it in every line of her body.

"What is your name?" he asked in Arabic. She remained silent. He lit a cigarette and inhaled, needing the stimulation, needing to think. He glanced around the room, knowing that he had to take his things just in case. He was throwing clothes into his bag when she replied.

"Jennifer Sheridan."

Holy shi—Quinn was glad he'd had his back to her when he heard her name. Otherwise she would have seen his reaction. No wonder she had looked familiar to him. What the hell was Senator Andrew Sheridan's daughter doing in Shiran of all places? God! That made the whole situation even more explosive. A senator's daughter as a hostage! When Omar's men messed up, they managed to do a hell of a job of it.

Since she thought he was a native, he gave no indication that the name meant anything to him.

"What are you doing in Shiran?" he asked, looking around the room to be sure he had everything.

"I'm working with the Feed the Children program."

"Where are your headquarters?"

"Sirocco."

"What were you doing this far south?"

"We were trying to scout out the needs of the outlying settlements."

He turned and looked at her. "And you discovered them, didn't you?'

She shuddered. She answered in English, no doubt figuring that her native captor would not understand her. "What I discovered was what a coward I am. I never realized that until today."

He answered her anyway, still in Arabic. "It is not cowardly to want to live, you know," he offered, wanting to reassure her for reasons he didn't understand.

She just shook her head, refusing to comment.

"Do you have a place to go if I release you?"

Her gaze flew to his face. "Are you going to let me go?"

"I've got to do something with you!"

"If I could get back to Sirocco..." Her voice died away.

"Do you know anyone in the small village where they found you?"

She shook her head. "No. That's the first time we'd been there."

"Hadn't you been warned that this area was dangerous?"

"Well, yes, of course, but we thought—"

"You didn't think at all, you were so busy trying to save the world!"

"Trying to save your people, you mean."

He just stared at her without answering.

"Why are you so angry?" she asked after a few moments of strained silence.

"Because your presence here has placed a great many plans in jeopardy. You have no idea what you have stumbled into."

"No. You're right."

"I've got to save your neck for you, putting my own in a noose doing it, and you're wondering why I'm angry?"

"Why do you feel you must save me?" she finally asked when he didn't say any more.

Quinn deliberately switched to English. "Allow me to introduce myself, Miss Sheridan. Major Quinn McNamara, USAF, at your service. I've been here for almost two years, attempting to infiltrate that little group you met tonight. But none of that matters now that you've waltzed onto the scene, does it? I've got to forget everything else and save Senator Sheridan's daughter's sweet little ass before her disappearance creates an international crisis."

Her look of relief was almost ludicrous. "An American! Oh, thank God!" Tears began to roll down her cheeks. He threw up his hands, grabbed his bag and walked out to the Jeep.

He tossed the bag into the Jeep, took one last drag from his cigarette, then ground it out with his heel. He looked up into the star-strewn night. Jennifer Sheridan. Not just any old tourist wandering around. It had to be a senator's daughter. He could already visualize the repercussions. Did Omar have any idea what kind of dynamite they were sitting on? Did Quinn dare tell him? He probably didn't know who she was and might wonder how Quinn knew.

Or he might decide to change his plans and hang on to her, in which case her life wouldn't be worth much at all.

There didn't seem to be any alternative. He was going to have to take her to Sirocco and go the most direct route—through the desert. He might be able to come back and tell Omar that he left her out there to die.

Omar might believe him. Few people survived that area, and Quinn sure as hell wasn't looking forward to the journey. But making the circuitous route would be unthinkable; they would be seen. It would be reported back to Omar, and he would know that Quinn had lied to him.

The only way to salvage the situation was to get her to Sirocco, come back and make up some tale to explain his delay in returning. In the meantime, he needed to gather some supplies to see them through.

The moon was coming up on the horizon, shedding light on the barren landscape. At least they would be able to see. If they traveled at night and stayed quiet through the hottest part of the day, they might make it. He didn't want to think about any complications that might arise.

He went back inside and helped himself to some supplies from his landlord. He left money to compensate. He just didn't have any more time to waste.

When Quinn walked back into his room, he found the woman asleep on his bed. Now that she knew he wasn't a terrorist intending to kill her, her exhaustion had overcome her fear. No doubt she could rest easily now, knowing that he was going to do what he could to get her back to safety.

His mind kept returning to the men who had been with her. Had they been killed? If not, would they set off an alarm that she was missing? More than likely. That's what he would do in their place. And there wasn't a damn thing he could do about it.

Quinn had long ago given up worrying about things he couldn't help. He was committed to getting this woman to Sirocco. Then he would have to deal with Omar. He hoped he could handle him. The Shiranese leader seemed to trust him, listen to his advice. Quinn would admit to a weakness for blondes, which would account for several days of his otherwise inexplicable absence.

In the meantime, they had to get on the road. He walked over to the bed and picked up the sleeping woman. She didn't stir. Shaking his head, he went out to the Jeep and placed her across the back seat, pillowed on the camping equipment he had helped himself to. The canvas tarp would help to keep the sun off them during the day.

He crawled into the driver's seat and lit a cigarette. It was going to be a long night. It would take several days to cross the hot expanse. He glanced over his shoulder at the woman still asleep behind him.

"I wonder what your daddy would do if he knew where you were at this very moment?" he muttered to himself. He had a hunch he knew. The man would come down on the Shiranese government like an avalanche in the Rockies.

Not that she cared. She was having too much fun rushing around trying to save the whole blooming world.

He followed the narrow track out into the desert. He wouldn't have to worry about traffic. His biggest concern would be following the track that could quickly become obliterated by the blowing sand.

Well, Max, here's a little monkey wrench thrown into our plans. Hope you approve of the way I'm handling this situation, he thought to himself.

He had a hunch that Max would have his head if he knew.

Two

―――

Jennifer shifted restlessly, trying to escape the heat that seemed to be baking her. She opened her eyes and stared at the canvas stretched a couple of feet above her. Turning her head, she looked at the man asleep beside her.

The heat didn't seem to bother him even though rivulets of moisture trickled down his forehead into his thick black hair. Some collected across his cheek-bones. She sighed. Nothing seemed to bother the man.

They had been traveling together for two nights and were now going into the second day, and she knew next to nothing about him except that he was angry with her for being in Shiran. She wasn't sure whether to believe what he had told her. A major in the air force, in Shiran? A man who looked like most of the inhabitants of the country, with black hair, a black beard and eyes equally dark—with a name like Quinn McNamara? He looked as though he had Arab blood in him.

She didn't remember much of their first night traveling. He had stopped once at a village and brought some clothing back to the Jeep. He hadn't wasted any time getting back on the rough road and putting as much distance as possible between them and any sign of civilization.

After the sun had come up, he had found them a place to camp, had fastened the canvas to the side of the Jeep, offered her food and examined her leg and cheek. All without saying a word.

Perhaps she had dreamed that he'd spoken in English to her that first night. Perhaps she was dreaming all of this. She was no longer sure about anything, except that whatever he'd put on her leg had brought the swelling down. He'd also spread some evil-smelling salve on her arms, legs and face, turning her skin an ugly mud color.

It was only when he had started pulling her hair out of its partial braid and putting the smelly salve into her hair that she had jerked away, protesting. Without saying a word, he'd pulled her back and continued to color her hair, ignoring her comments.

Jennifer had no strength to fight. She'd been in a state of shock since she, Randy and Paul had been stopped and questioned by men carrying automatic rifles. She'd watched in horror as her friends had resisted the challenge and attempted to ignore the men, only to be shot down and left for dead. She had known that she would suffer a similar fate and had prayed it would be as quick.

The next hours were a merciful blur. A confusion of images were all that she could remember, until a pair of black, angry eyes superimposed themselves over her memories. His eyes. She had thought about them while she had waited with the two men in the empty room. The expression in his eyes had stuck with her. Although all of the men's eyes were dark, the rest had been without expression. His eyes had been alive with anger and disgust.

And yet he was the one rescuing her. He was the one who had fed her, found her clothes more suitable for the desert, and tended her wounds. He was the one taking her across this broiling inferno of a country to safety.

Who was he, really, and why was he doing this? She had watched him these past few days and had wondered. But she hadn't asked.

All she knew was that for some reason she couldn't begin to understand or explain, she trusted him.

In looks he was very similar to the natives of the country—his skin burned a deep brown from the sun; his thick black hair and closely cropped beard like those of most men she had seen since arriving in Shiran. He was taller than some, close to six feet tall. His arms and shoulders were powerfully built, as though he was used to carrying heavy equipment.

She wondered what he looked like when he smiled.

She wondered if he ever smiled.

Jennifer shifted once again, trying to find a comfortable spot on the hard ground, wishing she could fall asleep again, wishing that when she awakened once more it would be cool enough to be bearable, cool enough so she didn't feel that the air actually singed her lungs when she inhaled it.

And yet she knew by now that once the sun was down, the air would turn cold and she would be glad for the voluminous djellabah and burnoose that her rescuer had tossed to her the first night.

He might not talk, but there was no doubt but that he knew what he was doing. He had a calm air of competency that Jennifer found soothing.

Her gaze returned to his profile. She wondered how old he was and how long he'd lived in Shiran and what he was doing there and why.

Why was he helping her? From the grim expression he wore, it wasn't out of a strong desire to know her better. In fact, he acted as though he disliked her. Perhaps it wasn't her. Perhaps he disliked all women. How could she possibly know? Without a doubt he was a man of few words. A man of mystery. Jennifer had never met another man like him.

Lying there under the protection of the canvas, trying to ignore the melting heat, Jennifer wondered if Randy and Paul had survived. Silent tears trickled down her cheeks. They hadn't deserved what happened to them.

What kind of world did we live in where people's lives were threatened, where they were shot, because they wanted to help starving children to survive?

Every time she closed her eyes, Jennifer's mind replayed the scene: the rifle-carrying men stopped them, forced Randy and Paul out of the truck and searched them. When her friends protested the treatment, the explosive sound of weapons rang out—

Her eyes flew open; she didn't want to remember anything more.

Jennifer wondered if she wouldn't have been better off dying then, rather then making this attempt to flee to safety. Where was safety anymore? Safety for whom?

Was it safe to be Senator Sheridan's daughter, but unsafe to be the hungry child of a local villager? What right did she have to unlimited food supplies when these small children had never known what it felt like to have enough to eat? Her friends had teased her about her social conscience. Whatever it was, she'd been driven to do what she could to help.

And she, along with the others, *had* made a difference in the eight months they had been in Shiran. Despite the bureaucratic red tape in both Washington and Shiran, the small group had managed to distribute food to families.

She had been able to see weeks-old infants thrive and grow strong and toddlers who had been too weak to walk slowly gather their strength until they could run. She now knew it to be fact: one person could make a difference if she chose to. As their group had come together in twos and threes, they had formed an international organization that slowly and inexorably pushed past the red tape and reached the people who desperately needed help.

She'd never been sorry she chose to come to this country. Given the same choices, she would do it all over again, even if it meant being with this stranger fleeing across the desert, even if it meant not surviving the trek. Coming here had been worthwhile because others now knew something could be done. She had given hope to people who had lost theirs. If she managed to get out of Shiran alive, she would work just as hard to continue the group's efforts, either in Shiran or Washington.

The trick was getting out alive.

Quinn sat quietly and watched the sleeping woman lying nearby. He needed to awaken her so that they could continue their trek to the coast, yet he hesitated to do so because she was resting so peacefully. The angle of the sun had lessened the intense heat, and a slight breeze playfully moved along the ground, teasing wisps of hair around her face and moving on.

Until now Quinn had never really studied her face. He had done everything he could to ignore her, ignore the fact she was a woman, an attractive woman, ignore the fact that he had been months without a woman. He could no longer pretend that he wasn't aware of her and her delicate beauty.

Since he'd put the cream on it, her hair looked more gray than blond, much less noticeable in case they were observed, but the color in no way detracted from her finely drawn features, the delicately arched brows, the long, thick lashes, the high cheekbones, the full, sensually shaped mouth. Even though she wore shapeless desert clothing, he knew that her slight small-boned body was softly rounded and contoured. He had held her in his arms.

She had amazed him these past two days with her stoicism. He had refused to talk to her except to give orders. He didn't want to say anything else until he got his temper under control. After all, it had been his choice to jeopardize the position he'd managed to attain in order to smuggle her safely out of the country. She hadn't asked him to. She had asked nothing of him. but he was having a tough time accepting his decision. Eighteen long months of intensive work had been put on hold because of this woman. Her very presence irritated him. Perhaps he'd wanted her to whine and complain, to ask questions, to demand answers, so that he could have vented some of his frustration on her.

She had done none of those things. She'd gone along with his terse directives without question. He had told her he would take her to Sirocco and get her out of the country. She had believed him.

He had seen her exhausted. He had seen her in pain. He had seen her sweltering in the heat. She had never shown her fear. Perhaps she didn't have sense enough to be afraid. Maybe she didn't understand the constant perils that accompanied their flight.

They could be stopped at any time and questioned. They could be taken into custody by the government now in power, which was not known for its humane methods of interrogation. Or they could be discovered by Omar's agents and returned to him to explain the reasons for their flight.

At the very least, she should be afraid of him, shouldn't she? How could she be certain that he wouldn't sexually assault her as payment for helping her to escape? And yet whenever she looked at him, her gaze was clear and steady, waiting for direction, seemingly willing to follow his lead.

He'd never met another woman like her. He found himself curious about her background. Her father was well-known. He'd been in the Senate for years. No doubt she had grown up used to politicians, diplomacy and strategic maneuvering for position. How had such a life affected her? And what in the hell was she doing in Shiran during such a time of unrest and instability?

His initial impression was of some bored debutante who had decided to play at saving the world. Now he wasn't so sure. He found himself unwillingly admiring her.

Quinn had met very few women whom he admired.

He glanced at his watch, then at the sun, and knew there was no more time to spare. He leaned over to shake Jennifer's shoulder, then paused. Instead he called her by name.

"Jennifer?"

Her eyes flew open, startled by the sound of her name. He had never used it before. "Yes?" she asked, pushing herself up and looking around apprehensively.

"I didn't mean to alarm you," Quinn said wryly. "It's time to leave now."

"Oh." She pulled the hood of her burnoose over her hair and crawled out from under the canvas that had provided protection from the sun. She motioned to the hillock that had provided them privacy earlier to answer nature's call. "Do I have time to..." She paused as though uncertain how to describe her needs.

He nodded and she hurried away without looking back.

How did she know he wouldn't go off and leave her there, he wondered. That was what Omar had expected, had planned for him to do, abandon her somewhere without hope of survival. He shook his head. Life seemed to have such little meaning in this part of the world.

By the time Jennifer returned, Quinn had the Jeep reloaded and was waiting behind the steering wheel. She ran the last part of the way and crawled into the passenger's seat breathlessly.

"There was no reason to run," he offered, starting the engine. "I don't intend to leave you."

She looked at him in surprise, and he realized she was startled because that was the first time he'd spoken to her since they'd begun their journey, except for direct commands. He sighed and faced the fact that, while she had slept and he had sat there thinking, he had come to terms with the choices he had made and was no longer angry. He had finally accepted their situation.

"I mentioned it the other night, but you may have forgotten. My name is Quinn McNamara," he offered in the way of conversation.

"I thought someone called you Rashid," she offered tentatively.

She was quick, he had to give her that.

"That's the name I've used in this country."

"Quinn McNamara," she repeated slowly, her gaze taking in his features and color of hair. Since he was talking, she decided to voice her doubts. "You don't look like a Quinn McNamara to me."

He laughed at the unexpectedness of her remark and found himself startled by the sound. He couldn't remember the last time he'd laughed at anything.

"True enough, but nevertheless, that's the name given to me by my Scots father and his Egyptian bride. Obviously I look more like my mother's people."

She nodded. "That explains a lot."

He shrugged. "I suppose." He reached into his pocket and pulled out a package of cigarettes. He offered her one, and she shook her head. He placed one in his mouth and stuck the package back in his pocket. "Good for you," he mumbled, lighting the cigarette. After inhaling, he removed it from his mouth. "It's a nasty habit."

"Then why do you smoke?"

He glanced at her from the corner of his eye. "I have several nasty habits. If I gave them up just because they weren't good for me..." He let his words die away and put the cigarette back in his mouth.

She smiled. She'd been astounded at how different he looked when he laughed, his white teeth flashing in the inky blackness of his beard. She was uncertain why he was talking with her after all this time, but was delighted. She'd been living with her own thoughts and feelings for so long. It was a relief to have some sort of distraction.

"Do you consider yourself Scots or Egyptian?" she finally asked when it became obvious he wasn't going to say anything more.

"Neither. I'm as American as apple pie, the Fourth of July and the Statue of Liberty."

She grinned. "That's pretty American, all right. If I might ask, what are you doing here in Shiran?"

"You can ask anything you want. Just don't always expect to get answers. How about you?"

"Me?"

"Yes. Whatever possessed you to come to Shiran to feed hungry children? I'm fairly certain you could have found them in many countries. Surely you must have known about the political situation here?"

"To a degree, I suppose. No one is ever fully aware of what's happening in another country, unless they've got a line into the intelligence community there." He turned sharply to see if that was supposed to be a dig at him, but she was looking straight ahead through the windshield and continued speaking. "I wanted to do something productive with my life. I wanted to make a difference, help people." She looked down to where she hung on to the bar beside the seat in order not to be bounced out of the Jeep. "I know that sounds corny and idealistic, but that's the only way I know to describe how I feel."

"How long have you been here?"

"Just over eight months."

"Eight months! I thought you'd just arrived!"

"Oh, no. Our base is in Sirocco, but we've set up distribution points in several areas where we truck the food in after it's shipped into the country."

"And you were looking for another distribution point when you were captured?"

"Yes. We'd never been this far south before. Randy and Paul thought it would be a good idea to check it out, only..."

"Only the three of you were checked out, instead."

"Yes."

"I'm sorry about your friends."

"Me, too. Do you suppose they survived the shooting?"

"I don't know. We may never know."

"That's the part that keeps playing through my mind. No one knows what happened to us. We were supposed to call headquarters. We called each night to report in. I know the people we've been working with must be frantic by now."

"Would they contact the authorities?"

"Oh, yes. I'm sure they would."

"The question is, which ones? Shiran's or ours?"

She looked at him with a puzzled expression. "What difference does it make? Both, I would imagine."

He sighed. "Probably. So we'll have another international incident on our hands, with the Shiranese government denying all knowledge of your whereabouts, which in this case happens to be true, and our diplomats not believing them."

"Then those men who stopped us were not part of this regime?"

"No."

"They were rebels."

"Yes."

"And you're working with the rebels."

"In a manner of speaking."

"Why?"

"Because that's what I'm here in the country to do."

"Oh." She sat in silence for a long time, thinking about all that he had said. And all that he had not said. He was an American air force officer, and yet he was working with the rebels in this country. What exactly was he doing?

Obviously he had no intention of telling her.

When the silence stretched on for several more miles, Jennifer finally asked, "Do you have any idea how long it will take us to reach the coast?"

"No. I've never traveled this way before. According to the rather primitive maps I've looked at, as long as we continue north, sooner or later we're going to hit the coast. How far we'll be from Sirocco at that point is anybody's guess."

"Aren't you afraid of being lost?"

He looked at her as though amused by her question. "Lady, I'm afraid of lots of things, being lost is just one of them."

She found his admission intriguing. "What are some of the other things you're afraid of?"

He shrugged his shoulders without taking his gaze off the road. "I've never bothered compiling a list. And with my imagination I manage to come up with new fears every day. Let's just say that I've learned to live with them, okay? How about you?"

"What about me?'

"What are you afraid of?"

She smiled. "Of running out of gas in the middle of the desert and having to walk to the coast, for one thing."

"Yeah, that one's crossed my mind a few times. Luckily, I've been able to buy plenty of fuel whenever we've come across a settlement. If our luck holds out, we shouldn't have any problems on that score. What else?"

Quinn discovered he was enjoying the conversation. It had been so long since he'd spoken English that it had taken him a few minutes to start thinking in his native tongue once again. It felt good. He was also enjoying Jennifer's comments. She was quick, he had to give her that. She didn't miss much.

He could tell that she was thinking over his last question. He didn't push her. They would be driving all night, mile after bumpy mile, and it wouldn't hurt to stretch the conversation some.

Finally she said, "I'm not really sure about my other fears. I suppose my greatest fear is that I'll go home and not be able to work with this project anymore. It's very important to me."

Her answer surprised him. "It must be. I would think that almost being shot, being captured and threatened with death might be enough to discourage some people from wanting to continue what you're doing."

"I suppose you're right."

"You suppose? You mean you don't agree?"

"It's not that. It's just that *somebody* has to do it. Somebody has to take chances and help these people. Somebody has to care that they have enough food to eat." She shifted in her seat, still hanging on tight. "You'd think the government would care about the people. That they would appreciate the offer of help."

"They didn't, though, did they?"

She shook her head. "No. It's really crazy. If we'd been bringing arms and ammunition into the country, they would have offered all sorts of assistance. But food? They couldn't be bothered. We couldn't even get an audience with the president to help us accelerate the distribution. He was unavailable."

"But you did it without them."

She looked up at him in surprise. "Well, of course we did. We had no other choice."

"You could have chosen to go home."

"And let all the food we'd gathered rot on the wharves?"

"It wouldn't be the first time, you know."

"Well, we weren't going to let it happen this time," she said fiercely.

Quinn smiled at her vehemence. It had never occurred to her and her group to give up and go home. Just as it never occurred to her to be frightened of him and his possible intentions. She believed in what she was doing, and she went steadily ahead with her plans. She believed him when he told her he'd help her get out of the country, and she voiced no fears that he wouldn't be able to do so.

Her indomitable will and her trust in him came close to frightening *him*.

"Do you have any brothers or sisters?" he finally asked, surprised to discover that he wanted to know more about her.

"I have two brothers, both older, both hoping to run for public office."

"Have they?"

"No. They're both practicing attorneys. One works for the public defender's office."

"Why aren't you married?"

"What makes you think I'm not?" she asked quickly.

He raised an eyebrow at her defensive tone. "Oh, I don't know. Somehow I can't imagine a husband allowing you to risk your neck like this."

"What do you mean, allow? Married or single, no one allows me to do anything. I do what I think is best."

"I just bet you do," he murmured.

"What did you say?"

"Nothing. So what does your husband think about your being in Shiran?"

A little sheepishly she admitted, "I'm not married."

His mouth quivered, but he managed to control his amusement. "I see."

"Does your wife know where you are?" she asked in an assertive tone of voice.

"Of course she does. I tell her everything. Isn't that what a husband does?"

"Oh," she said, frowning slightly. Why did his being married surprise her? She knew nothing about him, really. But for some reason Jennifer found it difficult to imagine him in a loving relationship with someone. He seemed too hard, somehow. Too cold, as though he'd never had to consider another person's opinion or feelings—only his own.

"How long have you been married?" she finally asked when it became obvious that he wasn't going to say anything more.

"I'm not married," he said after a long pause.

"But you just said—"

"No. *You* just said. I merely went along with it."

"Oh."

He grinned. "So here we are, two single Americans cast adrift in this sea of sand and silt and sun . . . alone . . . and single . . . lonely . . . and single . . .''

"No."

"No?"

"That's right. No."

"Just like that?"

"Just like that."

"And do you always get your own way?"

She refused to look at him, but she could feel the heat in her cheeks. "Always."

"Are you aware that I probably weigh twice as much as you do? I'm almost a foot taller, and I'm the one in charge on this trip."

"Within reason."

"I beg your pardon?"

"You're in charge, within reason. Should you become unreasonable, then you will no longer be in charge." She glanced at him out of the corner of her eye. "At least of me."

"I see," he said thoughtfully.

She hoped he did. She certainly wouldn't like the issue to be put to a test. Of course he could overpower her, take advantage of her, abuse her. But he wouldn't. He wasn't that sort of person. Was he? Why had he brought up the subject in the first place? She'd had no doubt that he would protect her from harm. Was she going to need protection from him?

"Are you teasing me?" she finally asked.

"Who, me?"

His innocence shone like a light from his pure countenance, and she grinned. "That's what I thought. What were you trying to do, see if you could stir up a few more fears in me?''

"It wouldn't hurt," he said, and she heard a certain grimness in his voice that had been absent before.

"What do you mean?"

"I mean that we are in a very provocative situation, a very dangerous situation, a very explosive situation. Just don't count on the fact that I'll always act the way your father or brothers would."

"Oh, come on. I'm not that naive, you know!" she replied irritably.

The Jeep came to an abrupt halt.

"I'm certainly glad to hear it," Quinn said grimly, hauling her into his arms. He lifted her chin and pressed his lips across hers.

Three

Quinn was pleased that the element of surprise was on his side. By the time Jennifer realized what he was doing, he had both her arms pinned between them and he was free to concentrate on the kiss.

The kiss had been motivated more by the wish to prove a point to Jennifer than it had been by any desire for intimacy with her. Despite her comment to the contrary, Quinn found that Miss Jennifer Sheridan was indeed quite naive and very, very innocent of the ways of the world. From their conversation, he discovered that it had never occurred to her that she would be sexually abused. Shot…maybe. Killed…a possibility. Used by one or more men to relieve their lust? From all indications, it had never entered her mind. No wonder she wasn't afraid of men. She'd never had any reason to develop a distrust of them.

No doubt her two older brothers had protected her as she was growing up. Her father's name had accomplished more of the same after she'd become an adult. Even the two men she'd been with at the time she was captured had probably been more like protective guardians than possible suitors.

How in the world had her family let her out of their sight? They must have been crazy!

While all of these thoughts were running through his head, Quinn was also aware of the woman he held closely in his arms. She was fighting him, wriggling her body and moving her head in an attempt to get away from him. She didn't have a chance in hell of getting away from him, he thought grimly.

He slipped his hand to the nape of her neck and held her there firmly while his mouth moved across hers, exploring, seeking her softness. When she clamped her lips firmly together, he contented himself by touching her lightly with his tongue, outlining the shape of her mouth. His mouth slid to her cheek, and he tasted the gritty sand they couldn't escape, as well as the slightly salty taste of her perspiration.

He continued to explore the contours of her face with his lips, lightly kissing the bruised area of her cheekbone, placing a kiss in front of her ear, along her brow, on her fluttering eyelid and downward, across her nose until he found her mouth again. This time it was not clamped shut. This time it was slightly opened as though she were trying to get more air to her lungs.

He took advantage of the moment and kissed her more thoroughly. Quinn forgot why he'd begun the kiss. He forgot that they were sitting in the middle of the desert roadway in the dark. He forgot that he had walked away from many months of work because of this woman.

Quinn forgot everything but the feelings she aroused within him.

Her body shook as though from a chill, and he could feel her heart pounding against his chest. He could understand those symptoms. He was experiencing them, too.

He held her even closer, his mouth taking possession of hers as though by right of ownership. His tongue darted inside like a marauding invader eager for new conquests.

She was no longer fighting him. She had grown limp in his arms, but he wouldn't release his grip on her. Instead he took advantage of her acquiescence to continue to taste, to explore, to conquer, to experience the wonder of this woman, this small slip of a person who had been thrown so unceremoniously into his life, whose very existence at the moment depended on him and his survival skills.

At long last he eased the pressure of his hold on her, reluctantly lifting his mouth from hers, staring at her in shocked surprise.

What the hell had just happened to him? He'd been trying to teach Jennifer Sheridan a lesson. Instead he'd learned something about himself. He had never felt like that with a woman. He'd never had such a sense of wonder and excitement, such a sense of protectiveness and gentleness sweep over him before.

Slowly her eyes opened and she stared up at him. When she saw him, her expression changed and she reached up and gave him a slap that made his head ring.

Jerking away from him, she sat up and looked out over the desert.

Well, he certainly couldn't say he didn't deserve that, Quinn thought ruefully, rubbing his stinging cheek.

"So now we know," he murmured, half to himself, starting the Jeep.

They rode for miles in silence. Quinn tried to bring his motives clearly into focus. He'd been trying to warn her, that's all. He'd wanted her to understand the dangers involved. He'd wanted her to be afraid—

What was he saying? He didn't want her afraid of him, did he? Was that what he'd been trying to accomplish? He darted a glance at her. She was leaning back in the seat with her eyes closed, but he could tell by the way she tightly grasped the bars on either side of the seat that she was not asleep. He needed to say something to her. But what? He needed to make some sort of explanation for his behavior, give her some reason.

He could think of nothing to say to explain what had just happened. Quinn wasn't sure he understood it himself.

They continued to follow the road north in silence, each lost in thought.

Jennifer felt numb. What had just happened had been so unexpected she hadn't known how to deal with it. If he'd wanted to make a point about her vulnerability where he was concerned, he'd made that point very well. She had been unable to move. With astonishing ease, he'd held her immobile while he had leisurely kissed her.

The slap had simply been a reflex action. So why had his kiss affected her so? She had been kissed before. She and Paul had struck up a friendship that had been gradually deepening, obviously heading to a more intimate relationship. Then why should Quinn's kiss have been so devastating to her?

She didn't know and she was afraid to find out. Something had happened tonight, something that she didn't understand. Did this mean that he expected a physical relationship with her while they were traveling, despite her adamant statements earlier? Was this his way of pointing out how little her opinion counted in the way of things?

The desert air continued to grow cooler and she shivered, pulling her garments closer around her. Never had Jennifer felt so alone and so vulnerable. If it had been Major Quinn McNamara's intent to point out some basic traumas for her to consider, he had certainly made his point. There was a great deal more in this world to fear than pain and death. She wondered how much she would have to endure.

They came upon a village just before dawn. Quinn stopped at one of the small dwellings and inquired about food and possible lodgings. He was directed to a small inn toward the center of town. No questions were asked when he inquired whether he could rent a couple of rooms for the day. There was also a promise of water for bathing, as well as fresh food.

He went outside to get Jennifer.

"We're staying here today," he said brusquely.

"Why?" she asked, although she was afraid she already knew.

"Because I've got to have some decent rest, that's why. I doubt that anyone's looking for us around here. They'll be watching the coastal towns if anyone has become suspicious of my disappearance. We both need to get cleaned up, get some fresh food and get some sleep."

"How many more days before we reach the coast?"

"If we make the same time we have, I'd say three. We're about halfway there."

"I see."

He reached into the Jeep and grasped her around the waist. "Come on. Let's get inside before it gets any later. I don't know about you, but I'm tired."

As soon as he touched her, he wished to hell he hadn't been so impatient and had allowed her to crawl out on her own. But it was too late. Her waist felt so small that he wondered if his hands would actually reach around it. She had caught her breath when he'd touched her, and he could tell that she was holding it, waiting to see what he was going to do next.

Not a damned thing! As soon as her feet touched the ground, he let go of her as though he'd burned his hands. Then he stepped back and motioned for her to go inside.

The building was cool, with circular fans stirring the air. They were shown upstairs and down a narrow hallway. Their rooms were across from each other. She looked at him uncertainly, and he almost smiled at the obviousness of the look. She was surprised that she wasn't sharing his bed, no doubt.

He wasn't interested in ravishing innocent maidens these days, and from her reaction to his kiss, he would guess that her experience didn't amount to much.

Quinn had never considered himself to be oversupplied with virtue and honorable traits, but he sure as hell wasn't the kind of man to take advantage of this type of situation. She didn't have a damn thing to worry about, despite the kiss they'd shared earlier. That had been a mistake. One he didn't intend repeating.

There was a bathroom of sorts at the end of the hall. The innkeeper promised to bring food to them, then disappeared down the hallway.

"Look, you go ahead and clean up. I'll find a less conspicuous place to leave the Jeep and be back up in a few minutes, all right?"

Her eyes never left his face during the entire time he spoke. Slowly she nodded.

He turned and walked away from her. Jennifer closed the door of her room and looked around.

She had nothing to change into, but it would feel good to bathe and feel clean again. With a surge of determination she opened the door and went down the hall to the bathroom. It contained an old tub that she began to fill with rather rusty warm water. At least there was soap. She scrubbed her hair and body, luxuriating in the sensation of being clean again. She dipped her head into the water repeatedly, first soaping, then rinsing her hair. When she finally got out, she found a towel and dried herself, then wrung her hair out until it no longer dripped.

She didn't even have a comb.

Jennifer pulled the djellabah over her head, and it wasn't until she raised her hands to her face that she realized she was crying. The tears ran down her face and she just stood there appalled.

Why was she crying now? What was wrong with her? She was tired, hungry and scared. But what else was new? She opened the door into the hallway and came to an abrupt halt. Quinn stood there waiting.

"What's wrong?" he demanded, staring at her intently.

She shrugged. "I don't have a comb."

He looked at her in disbelief. "You're crying because you don't have a *comb*?"

She wiped her eyes, furious with herself. "It's as good a reason to cry as any, I suppose."

"If I were you, I'd cry because you've just washed off all your disguise. We've got to do something with your hair and skin before the innkeeper gets back up here, or he might become inquisitive about the blond woman who's passing through."

She hadn't even noticed. It had felt so good to be clean again that she hadn't paid attention to the fact that the salve she'd been wearing was water soluble.

Quinn grabbed her hand and pulled her down the hallway and into her room. "Stay there. If the innkeeper comes back, keep the hood over your head. He'll expect you to be shy. I'll be back as soon as I can."

Within a few minutes after Quinn left, there was a soft tap at the door. Jennifer remembered to answer in Arabic.

A young woman came in, carrying a tray ladened with fruits, bread and cheese. Both women nodded as she set the tray down and departed.

Jennifer sat down on the edge of the bed and began to eat. It had been almost twenty-four hours since their last meal. When Quinn came back, she motioned for him to join her, which he did by sitting beside her on the narrow bed and reaching over her to the table that held the tray. They ate in silence for several minutes.

Finally Quinn said, "Here. I found you a comb. I want you to put this stuff on your face and arms and be sure to comb it through your hair again. Then try to get some sleep. I'll see you tonight." Without looking at her, he placed the items he'd mentioned on the table and walked out.

Jennifer just sat there, staring at the door after he left. He'd found her a comb. She'd been crying, supposedly because of her lack of a comb, and he had found her one.

But he hadn't touched her and he hadn't looked at her.

Jennifer reached for the comb and slowly began to pull it through her gnarled hair. She found it peaceful and very soothing to sit there with nothing to concentrate on, combing her waist-length tresses. It was a comforting, familiar rite, something positive to do that she could hang on to in a world that suddenly seemed to be frighteningly alien to her.

She was seeing this country through different eyes now, as though the scales had fallen away. She wasn't the pampered daughter of a high-ranking American official any longer. She wasn't a benevolent provider of food and nourishment to those in need.

She was a woman traveling with a man she didn't know, wasn't sure she wanted to know, but whose kiss had affected her as no one else's ever had. She no longer knew who she was. All she knew was that she was afraid—afraid to find out who she was, afraid not to find out, afraid that she might not know. She might be lost forever—lost in a sea of uncertainty and confusion, of chaos and explosive emotions.

Her safe little world was gone and, for the first time in her life, Jennifer was truly alone, with no one to rely on but herself.

Quinn sat in the tub, enjoying submerging himself in water, and went over his options. The more he considered them, the more positive he felt about his plans to convince Omar that he took a few days off before returning to the village and his work there.

It was true that he'd shown no interest in the native women. If he showed up after being missing for a week or so, would he be able to convince Omar that he couldn't resist the temptation to avail himself of the blond woman's charms before he disposed of her?

There was a strong possibility it might work. And that was enough to give him hope. All he had to do was get Jennifer to the coast, convince her to go home, and head south. There was no reason to abort his mission. There had been no sign that anyone was interested in either one of them.

He relaxed, reached over to his shirt pocket and dug out his battered pack of cigarettes. Lighting one, he exhaled with a sigh and leaned back in the tub. He felt good. He was tired, but that would soon be remedied. He'd eaten, he was clean, and in a few hours they would be headed north again.

He smiled and closed his eyes. What more could any man want?

The images that flickered across his mind were erotic. Visions of Jennifer without the concealing robes danced in his head. She was smiling at him, holding her arms out to him, obviously wanting him as she motioned to a pillow-strewn bed....

Damn! He sat up abruptly, stubbed his cigarette out, and climbed from the tub and pulled the plug. What the hell was the matter with him? She was a responsibility, a burden. Nothing more. He pulled on his pants, gathered up his clothes and strode out of the bathroom. He needed some rest.

Quinn paused outside her door and listened through the slatted partition. He heard no sounds from within. Hopefully she was asleep.

He opened his door and went inside. Jerking off his pants, he stretched out on the bed and was out in minutes.

Hours later Quinn opened his eyes to a darkened room. He blinked, surprised that it had grown so late. He fumbled for the light and looked at his watch. Damn. He hadn't meant to sleep so long.

He stretched, feeling the muscles in his body respond. Obviously he'd needed the rest. His body had demanded it. He wondered if Jennifer was still sleeping.

Jennifer. His mind suddenly recalled some of his dreams and he flinched. They had been very erotic and very vivid. He wished to hell his mind would stop playing games with him. There was no place for a woman like Jennifer in his life. He was a loner. He always had been.

Quinn barely remembered his father. He'd been a decorated war hero. The only things his son had of his father were a few pictures in an air force uniform and his medals. He had grown up thinking that he had to live up to his father in some way. That's why he'd gone into the service. Because of his looks and his skill with languages, he had been recruited into the intelligence branch and here he was.

His mother had raised him to be proud of being an American, but she had also wanted him to know about his Egyptian heritage. She had taught him about her family, their language and their culture, enough so that he'd been able to understand the thinking of the Arab nations, even when he didn't agree with them.

His mother had died before he finished high school, and Quinn had been alone ever since. He stood up and began to dress. He was used to being alone. He preferred his life that way, with no complications.

Quinn crossed the hall and tapped on Jennifer's door. There was no answer. Where the hell could she have gone? Hadn't he cautioned her about not being conspicuous? He tried the door and found it open. He paused just inside the room. She was still asleep, her hair spread out over the pillow.

The blond color was gone, but the thick fine mass of waves was still very attractive, as were her finely shaped features. He walked over to her.

"Jennifer?"

She didn't stir and he frowned. Beneath the brownish cream on her face she looked flush. He reached down and touched her cheek. She was burning up!

He knelt beside the bed and gently shook her. "Jennifer? Jennifer, it's me, Quinn. Wake up."

She moaned slightly and turned her head. Slowly her eyes opened and she stared at him from those deep pools of blue.

"Quinn?" she asked in a small voice.

"Aren't you feeling well?"

She started to lift her hand, then let it drop by her side as though she found the effort too much. "My head hurts. And it's so hot in here."

Actually it was cool, the thick walls having kept out the worst of the heat. A lazy ceiling fan had kept the air circulating. Quinn got up and went over to where a pitcher of water sat by a basin. He poured some of it out, picked up a soft cloth and returned to her side. Once again he knelt beside her and began to stroke her face with the cool water.

She sighed and turned her face toward him.

There was no denying that Jennifer was running a fever. Quinn knew he was going to have to decide what to do. Should he continue on the road with her, hoping she would feel better, or stay close to civilization in case she became worse? He didn't know what to do, and indecision irritated him.

"I have to do this, Andy, please give me some credit for thinking things through," Jennifer said in a clear voice.

"Andy? Who do you think you're talking to?"

"I know what Dad said, but I can't help it. Surely you and Roger know what he's like. I have to do this."

Quinn realized that she was no longer with him, but was replaying some scene from her past. She was becoming agitated and he spoke soothingly to her.

"It's okay, Jennifer. Everything's okay. Just relax."

His voice seemed to quiet her. He continued to bathe her face and neck, but as time passed he realized that she wasn't improving.

He finally went downstairs and asked if there was anyone with medical knowledge in the area. He explained what was happening, and eventually an elderly woman arrived and followed him back upstairs.

She checked Jennifer's eyes, her tongue, felt under her chin and nodded a few times, then she pulled out a vial of something from a voluminous bag she carried. "She is not used to our climate as yet and no doubt has been under some strain. This will help to bring down her fever." She gave him directions as to how much and how often to give her the medication and suggested that if her fever didn't go down, he should submerse her body in cool water.

By midnight Quinn was desperate. Relieved that no one else had need of the bathroom, he filled the tub, stripped Jennifer, wrapped her in her sheet and carried her down the hall.

She had slipped into unconsciousness, only rarely rousing, but when he lowered her into the water she fought him.

"I know, honey. This must feel like ice to you, but we have to get your temperature down. We can't have your blood boiling, you know."

He'd taken off his shirt to keep it dry and had placed his arm behind her shoulders to hold her in place. Quinn stroked her head and neck with the water-soaked cloth. Slowly she began to relax against him without opening her eyes.

He hadn't bothered about her modesty and only hoped that she didn't fully comprehend what was happening to her at the moment. Her small body was on display for him, but he was too worried about her to appreciate the view. He was concerned about her slenderness. She had no reserves to draw on, he was afraid. Even though she was small, her figure was well developed and in perfect proportion. She was a pint-sized Venus, he thought with a half smile. He doubted very much if she would appreciate the comparison.

When she began to shake, he lifted her from the tub and patted her dry with a towel. After carefully wrapping her in the sheet, he took her back to her room. She continued to shake and he looked around the room. There were no blankets of any kind. Slipping off his shoes, he slid onto the bed next to her and drew her into his arms, hoping that his body heat would help.

She drew in a deep breath, then slowly released it as she burrowed into his shoulder. He smiled and tucked her against his chest. He would lie there with her for a few moments, then go back to his room. Surely by morning she would be better.

He closed his eyes, just to rest them, and drifted off into a deep sleep.

Jennifer felt as though she were floating in a turquoise lagoon with a dazzling white beach nearby. Palm trees swayed gently in the breeze, and the sunlight touched her face with delicate rays.

She smiled. The heat of the desert was gone. The nightmare of Shiran was behind her. She was resting now in this beautiful lagoon with no one but Quinn.

Quinn? She frowned slightly. What was Quinn doing there in the lagoon with her? He stood in the water beside her, his tanned chest broad and muscular, smiling down at her. She couldn't imagine why he was there. He'd been so eager to get rid of her, eager to see the last of her. And yet . . .

He had kissed her once, awakening emotions that she'd never known existed. How had he known they were there?

He touched her on the shoulder, so lightly that she scarcely felt it, and smiled at her.

Funny, she wasn't used to seeing him smile, but when he did, it was as though the sun had burst through the clouds. She felt warmed by his smile. She put her arms around his neck and smiled back.

The water was deep but he held her firmly, his hands cupped beneath her hips so that she rested against him, enjoying his closeness, the feel of his body. She sighed and raised her lips to meet his.

Jennifer shifted slightly in bed and felt the warmth of a body stretched out beside her. Her eyes flew open and she blinked.

She was lying on her side facing Quinn, who was also on his side, facing her, with one leg thrown across her hips. His arm held her closely pressed against him. He was sound asleep.

Jennifer froze, trying to remember what he was doing there. She vaguely recalled him coming to her room and talking to her, but she'd had a pounding headache and had been so hot. She couldn't remember very much about it. He had bathed her face, she remembered that, and kept giving her something bitter from a spoon.

She suddenly realized that she was not wearing any clothes and that the sheet—the only thing protecting her—was around her waist. Her breasts were pressed intimately against Quinn's bare, hair-roughened chest, and her head was snuggled under his chin.

His deep, even breathing was the only indication she had that he was not aware of their position. What was he doing there? She glanced down and was relieved to see that he still wore his pants. She also recognized that he had her pinned quite nicely to him and the bed. She wasn't going anywhere until he decided to move.

Now what?

By all rights she should be hollering her head off. She had never been in such an intimate situation with anyone. So why didn't she feel threatened by Quinn's presence?

Her reaction, or lack of one, had something to do with her dream, the gentleness of his expression, his smile, and vague memories of his caring for her the night before.

All at once she recalled his putting her into freezing water, forcing her to stay in it while he stroked her body—her totally nude body.

She could feel a flush that must have started at her toes envelop her body. She pulled away from the heat of his chest and stared up into his face.

There were lines in his face that she hadn't noticed before, sun lines radiating from his eyes and others disappearing into his beard. She wondered if there were dimples hidden beneath that silky mass.

Reaching down, Jennifer began to tug the sheet up, hoping to cover her breasts before he awakened. However, her movements caused him to shift and stretch and she froze, watching his face.

Quinn's dream had him caught up in the enchantment of sensual delight until he realized that he was no longer dreaming. He had a woman clutched to him, his leg thrown across her. Warily he opened his eyes and saw a pair of clear blue eyes watching him with a hint of apprehension.

Oh, hell. Now what had he done? He raised his head slightly and realized that he had fallen asleep in Jennifer's room. He remembered that she'd been shaking with a chill and he'd crawled onto the bed with her. She was lying on one of his arms, which was now numb, while the other was tucked behind her holding her solidly against him. He lowered his eyes and realized the sheet was no longer a barrier between them. Jennifer's small yet perfectly shaped breasts rested against his chest.

For a moment Quinn felt like the one with the fever, before he resolutely pulled the sheet up between them, tucking it securely under her arms.

"How are you feeling?" he asked in a husky voice, brushing his hand against her cheek.

About what? she wondered fuzzily before she remembered her horrible headache the night before. "Much better, thank you," she responded politely.

They lay there a few inches apart, staring at each other. Then Quinn groaned and closed his eyes, blindly searching for her mouth.

Four

The remainder of Quinn's dream disappeared as he experienced the reality of Jennifer in his arms. She lay nestled against him, warm and soft, and her mouth felt the same way. She wasn't resisting him, not at all.

She felt so good to him, and when she stroked her fingers across his chest, he thought his heart would take off like a rocket. He enjoyed the way she fit against him, pressed so securely down his length. He moved his hand from behind her and stroked lightly from her waist to her breast. His fingers trembled with anticipation as he placed his palm around her breast, enjoying the way it swelled in his hand.

He brushed his fingers lightly across the tip, back and forth, delighting in its reaction to his touch.

Jennifer quivered and he paused, wanting the moment to go on but knowing that he couldn't allow it to. With reluctance Quinn raised his head and slowly opened his eyes.

"Good morning," he whispered, fully aware that his hand still firmly held her breast.

"Yes, it is."

"I'm glad your fever's gone," he whispered.

"Is it?" she asked with a hint of a smile.

He grinned. She certainly wasn't frightened of him, not now. "Actually, I think I may have caught it."

"Would you like me to sponge your body down with cold water?"

"You remember that, do you?"

"Only parts of it, I'm afraid."

"I was told that would help to bring your fever down."

"It must have worked."

"Actually, I think it chilled you. That's why I was holding you."

"I see. That was very thoughtful of you."

"Wasn't it?"

They lay there in each other's arms, looking at each other. Her mouth finally twitched, then a grin escaped him. They both began to laugh.

When she could draw breath, Jennifer said, "My savior," with a grin.

He had the grace to feel sheepish. "I meant well, you know."

"What about this morning?" she asked, her gaze resting on his hand until he slowly slid it away from her.

"That was just a friendly good-morning kiss."

"Hmm. I suppose you could look at it that way, if you tried hard enough."

His grin faded. "I don't intend to go any further with it."

She nodded. "Good for you."

"Are you making fun of me?"

"Not at all. I've just never been in this kind of situation before, and I'm not sure what to do."

"What do you mean?"

"I'm not used to being without clothes in the presence of another person, particularly a male person."

"Oh, that."

"Yes."

"Well, it's a little late to be modest with me, under the circumstances. Think of me as you would your doctor."

"That's hard to do. My doctor is a woman."

"Oh."

"Besides, that was a rather undoctorly kiss, you know."

"I was just checking to see if your fever had gone down."

"Either that, or you were determined to see if you could make it rise."

"Did I have any luck?"

She shoved against his chest, causing him almost to fall off the bed.

"Hey! That's no way to treat the person who gave up his rest to soothe your fevered brow," Quinn said with a grin. He sat up and reached for his shirt.

"It seemed to me that you were catching up on your rest well enough when I woke up this morning."

"You'd be surprised," he muttered, buttoning his shirt.

"Where are my clothes?" she asked, carefully arranging the sheet.

"Over there," he said with a nod. "I'll go downstairs and find some food for us if you think you're going to be all right."

"I'm fine," she said with a smile and watched him walk away.

The question was, was she really? She had known from the time she woke up and realized she was in Quinn's arms that she wanted to experience one of his kisses again, to see if she had imagined those new feelings that had erupted inside of her the first time.

One thing for certain, she hadn't imagined them. They seemed to have leaped into being as soon as his lips touched hers. How did he do that? she wondered whimsically.

She got up and quickly slipped on the djellabah, discovering that she wasn't as well as she first thought. Her head was swimming. Holding on to the wall, she followed the hallway down to the bathroom and tried to come to terms with herself and the situation.

Jennifer knew nothing about Quinn McNamara. Well, actually, she supposed she knew more than one might guess. He was tough, he was competent, but he could also be tender and caring. That was a great deal to know about a person.

But she knew nothing about his life, except that he obviously enjoyed danger. Otherwise he wouldn't be where he was, doing whatever it was he was doing.

He was pacing in her room when she returned. Whirling on his heel, he demanded, "Where the hell were you?"

"In the bathroom."

"Oh."

"Did you think I'd run away?"

"I didn't know what to think. Under all that junk you still look pale."

"I know. I don't tan."

"That's not what I mean. Are you sure you feel all right?"

"I'm okay. Just a little shaky."

He nodded toward a tray on the table. "There's something to eat if you want it."

"Have you eaten?"

"All I want."

"What are we going to do now?"

"That depends on you."

"What do you mean?"

"I had planned to travel all last night, but since we didn't, we could leave this morning, if you think you could handle traveling in the daytime."

She nodded. "It's important that we keep going as quickly as possible, isn't it?"

"Yes. But I don't want to make you worse."

"I'm sure I'll be all right."

She picked up the bread, goat cheese and handful of dates he had brought and wrapped them in the napkin that was lying nearby. "I'm ready."

"Are you sure?"

She nodded. She could always rest in the Jeep if she had to, she consoled herself.

When the sunlight hit her once more, she wasn't nearly so certain she'd made the right decision, but clamped her jaw and followed Quinn down the lane to where he'd parked the Jeep. The day was already hot, and the sun had only been up for a couple of hours.

As the day progressed, the heat grew more intense. Eventually Quinn realized they were going to have to stop and wait out the hottest part of the day. He started watching for any sign of vegetation or rocks that might shelter them. The next rise gave him an opportunity to look over the countryside, and in the distance he saw some greenery that looked to be shade of some sort. As they started down the other side, he kept his bearings, and within half an hour they came upon a stand of trees with abundant grass growing.

Knowing there must be water nearby, he pulled up and stopped, then looked at Jennifer. She still gripped the bars to hold on, but he could tell she was asleep.

Something in his chest seemed to ache as he looked at her. She had never once complained through any of this, even though the heat must be affecting her. He touched her forehead and was relieved to feel that it was moist and cool.

She opened her eyes. "Where are we?"

"I haven't a clue," he said, looking around. "All I know is that we're still headed north."

"Why are we stopping?"

"I saw this shade and thought we might enjoy it."

"Sounds good to me," she said, moving stiffly as she climbed out.

He got out and walked around the Jeep. Taking her arm, he led her to the center of the trees, where there was shade.

"Oh, look," Jennifer said, pointing. "Isn't that a spring?"

"It looks like one."

Quinn led the way to the water, which seemed to bubble out of the rocks and form a small pool, approximately ankle deep. He would test it to find out whether it was drinkable, but even if it wasn't, the area would provide some welcome shade and moisture.

A sudden breeze rustled through the trees and he glanced up. Usually at this time of day no air was stirring.

"Have you noticed? The sun isn't as bright as it was," Jennifer pointed out. "Or is it just because we're here in the shade?"

A premonition of disaster caused Quinn to sprint for the Jeep.

"What's wrong?" Jennifer cried.

As soon as he reached the Jeep he knew he hadn't been mistaken. He'd only seen one in his lifetime, but one was enough to enable him to understand the danger they were in.

"It's a dust storm, and it's rapidly heading this way," he shouted, grabbing the canvas, their canteens and the small ration of food. "Come on," he hollered above the wind that seemed to have appeared from out of nowhere. "Let's look for some shelter."

Near the spring was an outcropping of rock. Quinn hurriedly knelt down beside it and spread the canvas so that it could be pulled around them. Sitting down with his back against one of the large rocks, he yelled, "Come here, quickly!"

She scrambled down beside him, and he jerked her robes around her, pulling the hood down around her face. He emptied the napkin of food and doused it with water. "Put this over your face. Hurry." Then he took the food and stuffed it inside his jacket, rolling the garment tightly and placing it behind them.

He pulled the canvas around them so completely that there was no light, carefully making a fold over every glimmer.

"We won't be able to breathe."

"We've got a better chance of breathing in here than we would out there. That sand will suffocate you. Let's hope these rocks will take the brunt of it. We're lucky to be here in the trees and grass. If we'd been in the Jeep, we wouldn't have stood a chance."

He was yelling to be heard over the wind that seemed to be a constant roar now.

How quickly it had come up. Jennifer had been in a couple of storms in Sirocco but had never been on the plains during one. In the close quarters she could almost hear her heart pounding in her chest.

Quinn pulled her into his lap and pressed her head against his chest. "The damp cloth will help," he murmured.

"But you don't have one."

"No," he agreed. She could almost hear his smile. She lifted her head but couldn't see him.

"I'll share," she offered quietly.

There was a moment of silence, then he squeezed her tightly against him for a moment before letting go. "What a sweetheart you are," he said almost under his breath, but she heard him, despite the noise around them. Perhaps it was because her ear was resting against his chest.

"Why do you say that?"

He dropped his head so that he was speaking directly into her other ear. "Most women would be having hysterics about now."

"What good would that do?"

"None, believe me."

"Besides, you aren't scared."

"Are you kidding? I'm petrified."

Before she could say anything more, a roaring—like some giant train, or a tornado, or a thousand demons—filled the air all around them.

Jennifer couldn't seem to get her breath. She felt as though a layer of dust circled in the enclosed space where they clung to each other. She groped for the wet cloth and shakily raised it to her face. She could feel Quinn's hand helping her guide it.

Never had she experienced nature in this form, as though the wind was rushing everything out of its way, sweeping the land clean. The air swirled around the cluster of rocks, tearing at the feeble protection of cloth and canvas as though to mock their attempts to breathe and stay alive.

Quinn had understood the powerful force and had anchored the canvas firmly, wrapping the two of them so that their body weight kept the canvas closed.

Jennifer lost track of time. All she was aware of was the horrendous roar that never seemed to let up, that continued to howl at them, tug at them, seek out every crevice and crack.

Quinn felt her shaking in his arms and knew what she must be going through. This was the first one he'd experienced out in the open. He hoped to God it would be the last. He had heard of people disappearing, never to be seen again, no doubt buried by the fury of the wind and the sand. Others who had survived shared their secrets with friends and family. Thus, Quinn had been told what to do, what little could be done. Survival depended on how long the wind blew. If it blew too long, they would suffocate inside their canvas shelter. But it they opened the canvas while the wind was still blowing, the sand would quickly clog their mouths and noses.

He had plenty of time to think, sitting there, waiting. Quinn had always assumed he would die in the line of duty. He'd never thought about dying with his arms around a beautiful, very brave, young woman.

He thought back over his life and wondered what, if anything, he would have done differently. Would he have chosen another profession, perhaps? Learned to play tennis? Played golf on the weekends? Gone home each evening to a wife and children?

Even in his most vivid imaginings, Quinn couldn't see himself as a husband, nor could he see himself living with a woman. So why did it seem so natural to have Jennifer in his arms? In the several days they had been together, he'd grown used to her presence, and he knew that if they lived through this he would never forget her, never forget the way she felt curled up next to him, never forget the beauty of her body as he'd bathed her.

He must have blacked out, because the next thing Quinn was aware of was the lack of sound. He lifted his head and listened and heard nothing.

Jennifer was a deadweight in his arms, and he shifted awkwardly, pushing at the canvas covering them. It felt as though one of the rocks had fallen on them, but when he got some leverage and stiffened his arms, the cover fell open and rivers of sand and gravel poured in on them.

"Jennifer? Honey, are you okay?" He lifted her away from him and studied her face. The damp cloth had long since dried out and fallen away from her face. The darkening cream was gone and her pale skin showed all too clearly. His heart began to pound. He came to his knees, then to his feet and lifted her to his arms.

Quinn hurried over to the pool that was barely noticeable in the piles of sand and debris. Carefully using his hand to skim the dirt from the surface, he quickly wet the cloth and began to bathe her face.

Oh, dear God, was he too late? He felt for the pulse in her neck, his hand trembling so much he could scarcely find the pulse point. Then he waited, holding his breath.

A fluttery pulse became discernible and he felt suddenly light-headed with relief. She was alive. Thank God! He continued to bathe her face and her wrists, watching her worriedly.

His vigil was rewarded when he saw her eyelashes quiver, then open to reveal her beautiful clear eyes.

"This is getting to be a habit, you know," she managed to whisper in a hoarse voice.

"What is?" he asked, sounding just as bad.

"Your bathing me."

He attempted a smile. "I couldn't think of anything else to do."

She stared up at him with a slight smile on her face. "Your hair and beard are gray," she said with a sense of wonder in her voice.

He chuckled. "I'm not at all surprised. I feel like I've aged thirty years in the past few hours."

She touched his beard and a fine dust swirled in the air. She grinned. "You could use a little water, yourself," she teased.

He leaned back on his heels and looked at her, then shook his head. She had no idea how frightened he'd been for her. Perhaps it was just as well. He looked around the clearing. The grass was flattened and gray with silt. Tree limbs and rocks were scattered around the water hole.

But at least there was water available, still bubbling out of the rocks. And they were alive. Sometimes it was necessary to give thanks for some of the basics in life. Like air to breathe and water to drink.

Quinn stood up and started gathering some of the twigs and limbs. "I don't know about you, but I'm not ready to get out on the road again. Why don't we stay here for a few hours and get some rest before starting out again?"

"Whatever you say. Remember? You're the boss."

"Glad you reminded me. I'd forgotten."

He made his way to the Jeep and found it almost covered on one side with sand. What a mess. He decided to start shoveling before dark. Then he would start a fire, make up their bedrolls and get a few hours' rest.

Later Quinn decided that none of his plans ever seemed to work out the way they were supposed to. Tonight's plans were no exception.

Actually he did manage to uncover the Jeep and make sure that it ran. He also managed to kindle a fire that felt good in the late-evening air. But swirls of dust still eddied around them occasionally, causing them both to choke, and causing the ashes from the fire to dance in the air.

"Maybe the fire wasn't such a good idea," Quinn managed to say between coughs.

"The dust would still be blowing," Jennifer pointed out, wiping her streaming eyes.

They had eaten and Quinn had managed to wash most of the silt from his hair, face and beard, but he could still taste the grit in his teeth.

"I'm not sure we're going to get any rest if we stay here," he said in disgust, putting the fire out with scoops of sand.

Jennifer stood and pulled her hood around her, looking to see if they had left anything, when Quinn suddenly grabbed her arm and jerked her behind one of the boulders.

She started to ask him what was wrong, only to gasp when she saw that he was holding a pistol in his hand. He was looking toward the Jeep.

"Stay here," he said in a voice she'd never heard from him, and with those words he seemed to disappear into the darkness.

She hadn't heard a thing. What was going on? One minute they'd been amiably talking, and the next—

And the next Quinn had turned into a stranger, a very dangerous armed stranger. As much as Jennifer wanted to know what he'd heard, she realized she was more frightened of Quinn in that mood than she was of almost anything she could think of that might be lurking in the shadows.

What did that tell her about the man she was traveling with?

She heard a gunshot, then two more in quick succession and she cringed. Was Quinn hurt? What should she do? She stood there sandwiched in the crevice between two jutting rocks, paralyzed by the possibilities of what had just happened.

When a figure materialized out of the darkness, she almost screamed.

"Let's get out of here," Quinn said grimly.

"Quinn? Are you okay?"

"Come on. Let's go." He grabbed her arm, and she ran to keep up with his long strides. When they reached the Jeep, she saw distant movement as though sand swirled along the road from where they'd come.

Quinn almost threw her into the Jeep, then leaped around the front of it and was behind the steering wheel and starting the Jeep in the same motion. He shifted gears and shot out onto the road.

"What happened? Who was that?"

"Someone nosing around the Jeep, hoping to help themselves to some modern transportation." *I hope that's all they were looking for,* he added to himself.

"Who was doing the shooting?"

"They started it," he said with a touch of grim humor at the childlike explanation of his behavior.

"They? How many were there?"

"Three."

"Three! My God, Quinn, you could have been killed!"

"Thank you for pointing that out to me, Jennifer. It's a good thing I brought you along on this little expedition, so you could help me work out some of the subtleties."

"You're being sarcastic."

"Congratulations. You win the jackpot for guessing correctly once again."

"Why are you so angry?"

"Why the hell shouldn't I be? Do you have any idea what would have happened to us tonight if they'd managed to get away with this Jeep? We wouldn't have had a snowball's chance in Shiran to have gotten out of here. In case you haven't noticed, there aren't any corner 7-Eleven stores to walk to and phone for a cab!"

"Well, don't yell at me. Shiran's planning and zoning board didn't consult with me when they laid out this particular area of the country!"

He seemed to be hitting every hole and rut in the road and he was driving faster than normal, so Jennifer had to get a stranglehold on the bars by her seat to keep from bouncing out of the Jeep. That would probably suit him just fine.

All right, so he was angry. Why take it out on her? she asked herself furiously.

All right, so he was angry. Why take it out on her? he asked himself, feeling the frustration of shooting two men over something like transportation. They'd managed to come up silently on horseback. No doubt they were used to robbing unsuspecting people who stopped by the water hole. And he'd even lit a fire for them, signaling his presence.

God! How stupid could he get?

After a few miles his mind went back to the subject of the shooting, like a tongue probing the socket of a newly pulled tooth to see if it was still painful.

Had he killed them? He had no way of knowing. When the first one fired at him, his defense reflexes had kicked in and he had shot twice before he thought about what he was doing. They had both fallen, and the one holding the horses' reins had leaped on the back of one of the animals and taken off, leading the other two horses and leaving his fallen comrades.

Surely the man would go back and check on them. Maybe he'd only winged them. Maybe—

What the hell difference did it make? The deed was done. He was tired and he ached all over, particularly his left arm. He absently rubbed his upper arm and winced at the pain that shot down to his fingertips. He absently drew his fingers away from his arm. They were wet.

That certainly made an end to a perfect day. He'd been shot.

Five

———

Quinn lost track of time. He focused on keeping the Jeep on the road. He focused on continuing to head north. He tried not to focus on the ever-increasing pain in his arm.

It was interesting how the adrenaline that had been pumping through his body had kept him from feeling any pain when he was shot. He'd been hurt before. Knifed. He'd had the same reaction then.

Now he had plenty of time to be aware of his arm and the pain and to wonder what the hell he was going to do about it.

They had crossed the most arid part of the country. Surely they must be coming closer to civilization. They would soon start encountering more and more settlements. Perhaps in one of those villages he could find a way to get Jennifer back to her organization in Sirocco.

He didn't want to endanger her any more than he had to. Who could he trust? He wasn't sure anymore. It was hard to think when the pain got so intense. He thought about trying to find the words to describe what he was feeling, to see if that would lessen it. If he could describe the pain, perhaps he could contain it, make it go away.

Okay. So, uh, it was a throbbing pain, as though every beat of his heart sent out pulsations of red-hot shocks, and it was, uh, it was the length of his arm, and there was...damn, the bumps in the road didn't help anything, either...let's see, it was causing an aching in his shoulder that seemed to be—

Nope, that wasn't helping a thing. So, maybe what he needed was some distraction.

"Talk to me," he said, unaware of how grim and gruff he sounded.

Since they had been bouncing along for several hours in silence, Jennifer's surprise at his comment wasn't uncalled for.

"What about?"

"Anything. Your family."

"I've already told you about my family. Tell me about yours."

"What's there to tell?" he said through gritted teeth. He was going to have to slow down and try to miss some potholes. He had almost yelled when they hit that last one.

"Do you have any sisters?"

"Nope."

"Brothers?"

"Nope."

"A father? A mother?"

"Very cute. I told you about my father and mother."

"Oh, that's right. Did you get along with them?"

"I wasn't given a chance to get along with my father. He was a fighter pilot in Korea. He was killed when I was a baby."

"Oh, I'm sorry."

"You don't miss what you never had."

"I've never believed that myself."

"There have been a few times when I've doubted it, but it could have been worse, I guess."

"Were you close to your mother?"

"I suppose. She tried to do all the things with me that fathers would do. Went to all my ball games, that sort of thing."

"Did she ever remarry?"

"No. She said she'd never wanted another man after she lost my father." He grinned, thinking back. "But a lot of men wanted her, as I recall. She had the most beautiful black eyes, lovely skin and long silky black hair. She said my dad liked it long, so she never cut it, not as long as I knew her."

"She must have loved him very much."

He frowned. "But she couldn't let him go, you know? She wouldn't get on with her life. She might as well have died and been buried with him."

"But she raised you."

"Yes. Lamenting that I didn't look anything like the man she loved."

"How sad. You're an extremely attractive man. I wonder if she ever saw that?"

He glanced at her and grinned. "Thank you for the kind words. I'm touched."

"You should be. I don't hand out many compliments." She was quiet for a minute, then chuckled. "Notice I haven't said a word about your disposition. Just your looks."

He laughed, then gasped.

"What's the matter?"

"Nothing. I'm just getting tired. I don't suppose you know how to drive one of these things, do you?"

She looked at the foot pedals a little distastefully. "I suppose I could if I had to, but I've never felt an affinity for clutches. I don't understand them and they don't understand me." She glanced back at him. "Why, are you getting tired?"

"A little, but I can wait. I've decided to stop at the next settlement we come to and see what I can find out about getting you a ride to Sirocco. We can't be over a day or two away from the coast. If I can find someone that looks reliable—"

"I thought you were going to take me to Sirocco."

"There's no point in that. We've put most of the desert between us and the men who captured you. Nobody's going to be looking for you this far north. In fact, we could probably call your group and see about getting some transportation from them. Yeah, that sounds good. Much more dependable.''

Jennifer felt a sharp pain in her chest at his words. He was anxious, actually eager, to see the last of her, as though these past few days they'd shared meant nothing to him.

But then, what had she expected? A vow of eternal love or something? They were strangers, after all. *Strangers who had slept together, who had survived a dust storm together, who'd shared a midnight healing bath together....*

She had forgotten her real reason for being in Shiran, and that was not to become infatuated with an ill-tempered, mean-talking... fascinating, attractive...

"That sounds fine with me," she said tersely.

There was nothing more to be said.

They arrived in the village of Hidaj about mid-morning. Jennifer recognized it with relief. She had been there several times and had gotten acquainted with a few of the mothers of small children.

The drive had been long and something of an endurance test for her. Now that she knew how eager Quinn was to get rid of her, she felt as though she wanted to shrink and disappear. After their less-than-pleasant first hours together, he had seemed to accept the fact that they would be together for a few days. Well, the few days were up, and he was obviously chomping at the bit to get rid of her.

She had refused to look at him in the light that preceded the dawn. She knew what he looked like. She didn't want to be reminded. In fact, she was going to do everything in her power to forget the man as soon as possible.

But when she first recognized Hidaj, she turned to him, and said, "This is Hidaj! I know this village. You can just—" She stared at him in dismay. He was a pasty gray color under his tan, and his forehead was beaded in perspiration.

"What's wrong?"

"Not a damn thing," he said without looking at her. "So you know this place. That's great. Is there any place I can drop you off?"

She leaned closer to him. "You don't look so good, Quinn. Are you feverish?" She started to touch his forehead, but he jerked his head away.

"Do me a favor, will you? I'm a big boy now. I can certainly take care of myself, okay?"

"Fine."

"Now. Where do I take you?"

"Let me off right now. I can find my own way."

"That's cute. That's really cute," he muttered, shifting gears and slowing down for the traffic that was moving along the roadway.

"Look, I don't know what I did or said, but whatever it is, I'm sorry, okay?" She gazed straight ahead, looking for landmarks. "I thought we'd become friends these past few days. If I've offended you or something—"

"You haven't offended me, lady. Believe me. You haven't offended me. Look, I've enjoyed getting to know you, too. However, I'm not here for socializing. I've got work to do and it's back south a few hundred miles, so if you don't mind, I'd like to find a safe place to leave you and get back to what I was doing."

"Right. You might miss a few innocent tourists that you can shoot up or capture!"

He turned his black gaze on her without saying a word, then returned his eyes to the road.

Jennifer burst into tears. "I'm sorry. I didn't mean that! I don't know what's the matter with me. I've never been so rude with anyone before I met you. I've never behaved toward anyone the way I have toward you. I can't explain it, but I *am* sorry."

"Forget it. You've been through a rough time and you've handled it fine. Just fine." He didn't look at her. "It's nothing to cry about."

"I'm going to miss you," she said in a small voice.

He gave a humorless laugh. "That I believe. You'll miss me like a toothache, I'm sure."

She glanced up and recognized a street. "Oh. Turn right. About four or five blocks from here, there's a family that has been helping us distribute the food. They'll know when the next shipment is due. I can get a ride to Sirocco then."

Without saying anything, he turned the wheel and drove down the street she indicated. All of his movements were labored, as though his muscles ached.

"Why don't you get some rest before you head back?"

"I've got some things to do first. Maybe later."

"I'm sure Haida would be glad to have you stay with her family. They have a couple of extra rooms that we stay in whenever we're here."

He just shook his head.

Damn him, anyway. Why did he have to be so churlish? "Here's the house," she said, pointing. Quinn pulled up under an olive tree. He didn't turn off the engine, but just sat there waiting for her to get out.

"Aren't you even coming in?"

"I don't have to walk you to the door, surely. You're a big girl. Besides, you know these people. I don't."

She couldn't believe him. She really couldn't. She stared at him and once again was shocked by his lack of color. He was ill. He was really ill, and he intended to drive off and leave her as though nothing were wrong.

She must have given him her fever. That was it! And he didn't want her to know, so he was going to just drive away, drive out of her life, and she'd never know how he was doing, or if he was feeling any better or—

Jennifer reached over and, with a quick twist of her wrist, jerked the key out of the ignition. The engine shuddered to a stop.

"What the hell did you do that for!" he demanded.

Jennifer calmly got out of the Jeep and walked around to the driver's side. "Get out."

"Now see here—"

"No, *you* see here," she said, reaching for him. "I'm tired of this macho act of yours." Then she touched his arm.

And just to prove her wrong in her estimate of his manly ways, Quinn fainted for the first time in his life.

Someone was taking off his arm, Quinn decided—with a vice, twisting it tighter and tighter on his arm until he thought he was going to scream. He tried to get away, but they were holding him down.

And they branded him with a red-hot poker.

That's all he remembered.

Sometime later he was aware of voices and a soft cool cloth touching him, soothing his heated body.

His arm hurt. Damn it. What had they done to his arm? If they had taken it off, why the hell did it hurt so badly? He'd heard of that before. Yeah. Even after an arm or a leg was gone, men sometimes could feel them. They itched or something. Hell, his didn't itch. It burned like the fires of hell.

What were they doing to him?

"Just lie still now, Quinn. Everything's going to be all right. The doctor removed the bullet. He can't believe that you drove us here with a bullet in your arm. You did just fine, love, just fine."

Who was that? Who was calling him "love"? He wasn't anybody's love. Never had been. Never would be. He could never be the man his mother loved. But he had tried. He'd really tried. He'd wanted her to be proud of him. He'd wanted her to say, "You're just like your dad." She never did. She never did. Instead, she died. She probably wanted to die. Then they could be together.

He had no one. He didn't need anyone. He was just fine on his own.

"Here, love, open your mouth. This is some broth that will help you keep your strength. Just a taste, okay? For me? Please?"

There she was again, tormenting him with her soft voice and softer hands. Maybe she'd go away if he'd do what she said. Maybe she would leave him alone.

Damn, she smelled good. What was it she wore that smelled so good? Was that her hair that brushed against his cheek? He'd open his eyes in a minute and find out. In just a minute, he'd open his eyes. But not right now. He was so tired right now. He thought he'd sleep a little while before he opened his eyes to see who she was . . . or what she was.

When Quinn finally opened his eyes, the room was filled with flickering shadows and he realized that there was a small fire in a grate nearby. He had no idea where he was. Even worse, he didn't particularly care.

They must have given him something for pain. He couldn't feel his arm at all. That must mean they took it off. But then he couldn't really feel much of anything, except that he was floating several inches off the bed, which wasn't a bad way to travel, really. It sure beat the hell out of those interior roads.

His gaze lazily took in the room until he saw that he was not alone. A young woman in a thin robe, with long blond hair falling over her shoulders, sat curled up in a chair next to his bed. Her head was resting on the back of the chair and her eyes were closed.

"Jennifer?" he whispered in disbelief.

Her eyes flew open and she leaned forward, touching his forehead. She smiled. "Your fever has gone down. Good."

"What are you doing here?" He couldn't seem to find his voice. His throat was almost as dry as it had been after the dust storm.

She reached for a glass of water, slipped her arm under his head and raised it, then tilted the glass toward his mouth. She waited until he drank before she answered him. "I'm looking after you, what else?"

He looked around the room again and back at her. "How long have I been here?"

"Three days."

He closed his eyes in despair. Three days. He'd lost three days. Would Omar ever believe that—

"Quinn. You could have died. Your arm was infected. You could have lost it. Don't you understand? You've been really ill."

He could well believe that. He didn't feel as though he had the strength to lift his hand. He decided to experiment by lifting his right hand, then he looked at his left hand and said, "My arm's still there," in pleased surprise.

"Well, of course it's there. Minus the bullet that was lodged in it, of course. Where else would you expect to find your arm, anyway?" she said with a grin.

"I guess I must have dreamed it. I thought they cut it off."

"It may have felt that way. It was really inflamed by the time the doctor got hold of you." She took his right hand. "Quinn, why didn't you tell me you'd been shot?"

"No need to."

"Have to protect the frail little lady, I take it. The code of the swashbuckler or something, right?"

He smiled at her disgusted tone. "If John Wayne could do it, I can do it," he agreed.

She made a face at him. "Are you hungry?"

He shook his head. "What time is it?"

"About one o'clock."

"Where are we?"

"This is Haida's home."

"Did you contact your group?"

"Yes. I'm so glad I called. They were all frantic. Both Randy and Paul were taken back to Sirocco."

"Then they weren't killed."

"No. Thank God, although Randy was seriously wounded."

"That will teach them to go nosing around where they don't belong."

"Are you trying to start a fight?"

"Who, me?"

"Look, why don't we agree to disagree on this particular subject, okay? It is my firm belief that the first way to insure peace in this world is to see that everyone has enough to eat. Obviously you believe the only way to insure peace is to shoot everybody who doesn't agree with you."

"I wouldn't say that, exactly."

"Then what would you say, exactly?"

"I just have a more realistic attitude toward the world, that's all."

"That's a matter of opinion. And in my opinion, shooting people in the name of peace is like—is like—"

"Yes?" he asked. "Go on."

"Well, it's like having intercourse in the name of chastity!"

Quinn began to laugh, wincing with the movement of his arm, and watched with a great deal of pleasure as a bright rosy color covered her neck and face.

"I've never been a particular proponent for chastity, myself," he admitted when he stopped chuckling.

"I'm serious!"

"Yes, I know. You're so serious you almost got yourself killed. Do you have any idea what would have happened to you if I hadn't volunteered to, uh, dispose of you?"

"I would have been killed," she stated baldly.

"Yes. You would have. Eventually. But by the time they got around to killing you, you would have been begging them for that particular release."

"The whole world is crazy, just crazy."

"I'm not arguing with you on that point. I'm just trying to get you to look at where you are and what you're trying to accomplish. Your aims are laudable but a little impractical. At least, at the moment."

"What do you mean, at the moment? What's happening?"

"Look, I can't talk to you about it, all right? Just take my word for it that the next several months things in this country are going to get pretty sticky, and you and your friends are only going to come to grief if you insist on staying here."

"So you think we should just pack up and forget about all the children who need food?"

"Not forget them, no. But find local people to distribute the food once it arrives in Sirocco."

"Aha. You see, that's exactly what we've been doing. That's what we were doing when we were stopped by your men."

"They weren't *my* men, as you put it."

"Well, you're working with them."

"And for that you should get down on your knees every night and thank God."

Very quietly she said, "I have."

They stared at each other in silence for a long time until he finally closed his eyes.

There was no talking to the woman. He'd done everything he could to help her, but he couldn't stop her from going out again. Only the next time, he wouldn't be there to save her.

"Quinn?"

He didn't open his eyes. "What?"

"I really do appreciate all you've done for me."

"You're welcome."

"I mean it. You've risked your life for me."

"Good night, Jennifer. Why don't you go on to bed now?"

He heard her move from the chair, but wasn't expecting to feel her lips touching his. He opened his eyes and saw that her hair was hanging down on each side of them, like a curtain hiding them from the rest of the world. And then he closed his eyes again because her kiss was creating a commotion within him that he had to deal with.

He raised his right hand and slid it around the nape of her neck, and she sank down on the bed beside him, careful not to touch his left arm. Her kiss was feather light, so soft and gentle that he felt as though he'd been brushed by butterfly wings.

Her hands slid along his chin, cupping his face. When he deepened the kiss, her fingers moved over his ears and into his hair, loving the soft texture, the rich, inky blackness that she'd made excuses to touch while he'd been so ill.

When he nudged her lips apart with his tongue, she willingly allowed him entrance, greeting him joyously with her own. When she eased the pressure and attempted to pull away, he wouldn't let her, but kept his hand firmly against her neck.

He seemed to enjoy her response, coaxing her to explore with him, teasing her into following his lead, then showing her the provocative rhythm that would bring both of them so much pleasure.

Then his arm dropped away and he groaned. She quickly straightened. "I'm sorry. Did I hurt you?"

The grin he gave her was so sexually charged that she felt singed with the heat of it. "Let's just say you haven't done anything to my arm."

"Oh." Even though she could feel her face heat up, she refused to drop her gaze from his. He had the most beautiful eyes. They sparkled in the firelight and were filled with all sorts of suggestions that made her heart race. "I'd better let you get some sleep."

"That would be the safest thing at the moment."

She stood up and looked at him, wanting so much to lie down beside him and love him. But the doctor had him on fairly strong medication and it wasn't fair to take advantage of him. He was probably too weak to—

Her eyes fell on the covers that stretched over him and she realized that he wasn't as weak as she thought. Even so—

"Good night, Quinn."

"Good night, Jennifer."

He waited for her to leave the room. Instead she went behind him and began making some rustling movements, then grew quiet. He couldn't see her without turning around, so he asked, "What are you doing?"

"Going to sleep."

"In here?"

"Of course. I've been sleeping in here since we arrived."

He sighed. Just what he needed. "What does your friend Haida think about that?"

"It was her idea. After all, someone needed to be here with you."

"I suppose." After a moment he added, "But tomorrow I'm heading south."

His words circled the room, around and around, until they seemed to fill it.

Finally he muttered, "I have to. Don't you understand?"

"No. But I'll accept your word for it."

Damn. "Look, I really appreciate what you've done for me. I wasn't in any condition to thank you before. Hell! I don't even remember how I got here."

"I took the Jeep key away from you."

He laughed, wishing he could see her face. "I don't remember that. Rather clever of you."

"I was desperate. I knew something was wrong. I thought you had caught my fever."

"Too bad I didn't. Maybe you could have bathed me like I did you."

"What makes you think I haven't?"

She was kidding. Of course she was. No doubt there were several people in this household. Probably one of the men bathed him whenever he needed it. He remembered soft hands stoking his body. Surely that wasn't—

"Jennifer?"

"Yes?"

"Did you really bathe me?"

"Uh-huh. And that reminds me of something I wanted to ask you. What is that scar on your lower abdomen area? It looks like you were stabbed or something."

Dear God, she hadn't been kidding. A couple of inches lower and that knife would have taken care of a lot of things for him, including the uncomfortable sensation he was dealing with at the moment.

"Good night, Jennifer."

"Good night, Quinn."

He could hear the amusement in her voice. Damn woman, anyway. Thinks she's so smart.

It was a good thing for both of them that he was leaving tomorrow.

Six

___

The next morning when Jennifer walked into the small room where she and Quinn had been sleeping, she found him standing at the window looking out, a sheet wrapped around his waist.

"Good morning," she said, admiring the sight of his broad tanned shoulders and the narrowness of his waistline. His white bandage was a startling contrast to his sun-darkened skin.

He spun around at the sound of her voice and glared at her.

"Where the hell are my clothes?"

"I slept very well, thank you. And you?"

"And my cigarettes."

"I thought you gave up smoking," she commented, walking over to his bed and straightening the remaining covers.

"Whatever gave you that idea?"

She shrugged, not looking at him. "I would think it obvious. You haven't smoked for over four days."

"That's because I was unconscious for three of them," he replied in a wry tone, running his hand through his already rumpled hair.

Jennifer had a sudden vision of how his young son might look the first thing in the morning, particularly if he'd had bad dreams the night before. She smiled at the thought as she attempted to placate him. "See what a great start you've made? You're already well on your way to getting the nicotine out of your system."

He stared at her in silence for a moment. "Jennifer, don't you have enough to do saving the world? You don't have to save me, too." He yanked on the trailing sheet and strode over to her. "I want my clothes . . . *and* my cigarettes. Now."

She hadn't expected him to be pleased with his situation. He was a man who wanted, no, insisted, on being in control at all times. He must find his present predicament frustrating.

"The doctor is here to check your arm."

"Damn it! Have you heard a thing I've said?"

"Certainly. I'm not deaf. The entire household has no doubt heard you." She turned on her heel and walked to the door. Pausing in the doorway, she asked, "Are you always this much fun in the mornings?'' and closed the door before he could respond to her cheekiness.

Smart-mouth female. Quinn paced back to the window and stared blindly out. He didn't need the damn doctor pinching and poking his arm. What he needed was his clothes and a cigarette—not necessarily in that order—and then he needed to get the hell out of there.

The trouble was that he didn't want to leave Jennifer.

He must be losing his mind. He'd done what he set out to do—he had gotten her to safety of sorts. He couldn't force her to go back to the States. He was hoping that her father would do that. Her father had more rights over her than he did. Maybe her father could talk some sense into her stubborn head. If he could, more power to him.

Quinn had awakened that morning tasting her on his lips, which immediately had brought on the same symptoms he'd fought the night before when she had kissed him. Only now whatever they had given him for pain had worn off and his arm was aching, as well.

Finding his clothes gone had been the final straw.

The door opened again and a young Shiranese male came into the room.

''Good morning,'' he said in heavily accented English. ''It is good to see you awake after all this time. You are feeling some better?''

Quinn answered him in the man's own language and received a grateful smile.

''I'm fine,'' Quinn groused. ''I need to leave.''

The doctor nodded several times. "Yes, yes, I understand your impatience. If I might look at your arm first, please. It is necessary to change the dressing and make sure the infection is clearing up. It was severe. We have been giving you medication to help heal you more quickly."

He nodded toward the door. Quinn glanced over and saw Jennifer standing there holding his neatly pressed clothes, a dark bottle of what was probably foul-tasting medicine, and his cigarettes.

Without meeting her eyes, Quinn walked over to her and took everything out of her hands. "Thanks," he muttered ungraciously. Then, with as much dignity as he could manage with his hands full and wrapped in a bed sheet, he strode over to the bed and sat down. After placing the clothes on the bed and the medicine on the night table, he lit a cigarette and held out his arm to the doctor in resignation.

He inhaled on the cigarette and choked. "What's wrong with these?" he asked when he could get his breath.

"What do you mean?" Jennifer responded, puzzled.

"They taste awful!" He made a face and held the cigarette under his nose and sniffed.

"Yes, I know, but then they always have," she pointed out. "You have just gotten used to them." She walked over and picked up the bottle he'd set on the table beside the bed. "Here. Take your medicine and I'll bring you something to eat. You can't travel on an empty stomach."

"It wouldn't be the first time."

"Perhaps that's true, but there's no necessity for it today," she offered with a hint of impatience.

Jennifer measured out a large spoonful of the liquid and held it out to him. He had a vague memory of having done this before. He opened his mouth, took the medicine and swallowed it obediently, glaring at her. Her smile was as loving as a mother's to her three-year-old, he decided resentfully.

By the time the doctor had changed the dressing, Jennifer was back with a heavily laden tray. Quinn began to eat and realized that he wasn't as strong as he had first thought but was considerably more hungry. He leaned back on his pillow and rested between portions of food. Both the doctor and Jennifer had left. Not that he blamed them. Once again he'd been taking his bad mood out on everybody else.

He shook his head. Damn, but he was tired. However, the throbbing ache in his arm and shoulder was easing. The medicine must be working. He felt lighter, somehow. If only he didn't feel so sleepy.

Quinn yawned, then looked over at the tray. He'd made considerable inroads in the food Jennifer had brought to him.

He laid his head back on the pillow and sighed, stretching his legs out on the bed. He needed to get dressed now. Had to get on the road. His eyelids drooped. He might just lie there for a minute or so and let his breakfast settle. Maybe rest his eyes. Just for a few minutes.

He was sound asleep when Jennifer came in for the tray. She smiled, draped the sheet more comfortably around him and left the room.

The doctor said another day and he would be well on the road to recovery. She had done all she could do to get him there. After today he would be on his own.

So would she.

When Quinn again opened his eyes, he was disoriented. He'd planned to rest for a few minutes, then leave. However, the sun was no longer coming in through the window, which meant that more than a few minutes had passed.

What time was it? He raised his arm and noted that his hand was trembling. It was almost three o'clock. He glanced back at the window. It must be afternoon.

The door opened quietly and Jennifer peeked in. "Good," she said, coming into the room. "You're awake. Would you like something to drink...or eat?"

She looked young and very beautiful in a colorful flowing kaftan. She had braided her hair in a single thick braid that was draped over one shoulder.

He'd noticed earlier that the bruise on her cheek was almost gone, leaving her soft glowing skin without a blemish to mar its silky sheen.

"I'm sorry," he said quietly.

She looked startled. "For what?"

"For my behavior earlier. It was rude and uncalled for."

She nodded. "That's true. However, I've been around my dad and two brothers enough when they were sick or injured to know that most men don't take kindly to a sickroom."

"That doesn't excuse my behavior."

"I agree," she replied with an impish smile, "but it makes it much more understandable." She sat down on the side of the bed and caressed his cheek as though unaware of her actions. He was very aware of her—the floral scent that called her to mind as soon as he caught a whiff of it, the way her soft hand felt against his face. "What would you like?" she asked.

He almost told her.

Quinn cleared his throat. "Uh, some water would be fine. Anything liquid."

"And you need some more medicine."

He shook his head. "I need to go, Jennifer. I really do appreciate everything you and your friends have done, but I must get back."

"I know. But one more night would give you added strength, and you need your stamina. We both know that what you're doing is hard on you. You must be physically fit."

When he didn't say anything, she stood. "I'll be right back."

While she was gone, he lay there looking at the window, trying to piece together exactly what had happened to him this week. Somehow, without his knowing it, she had managed to get past all of his defenses and had touched his heart. He wasn't sure how she had done it. And he had no idea how to handle the situation.

They were from two different worlds in so many ways—socially, ideologically. They had nothing at all in common. And yet there was something between them, something he couldn't quite find the words to describe.

He admired her courage and her ability to cope with unexpected changes. He admired her spirit. She never backed down from him and gave as good as she got. He had seen her dry-eyed after having been captured and witnessing her friends being shot, dry-eyed when they'd almost lost their lives in a desert storm, and yet she'd cried because she didn't have a comb.

A bundle of contradictions, Miss Jennifer Sheridan.

He'd seen her laughing and in tears, tender and exasperated, and he'd seen her blush more than once. It was as though she had no fears about allowing him to see exactly who she was. Perhaps because she was comfortable with herself.

Yet for all her practicality, she was an idealist, dreaming of a new and perfect world where no one was hurt or killed, where everyone had enough food, where there was no greed or anger, but only peace and harmony.

He wished he could believe in such a world. It would be a marvelous place to live...and love...and raise happy, healthy children...who all happened to look like her.

Quinn groaned and covered his eyes with his good arm. This medicine must be making him drunk. He was fantasizing now, something he rarely did and never with a flesh-and-blood person in mind.

"Here you are," she said from the doorway, pushing the door wider with the tray. "I raided the kitchen. I wasn't sure what would look good to you."

He sat up and winced. His arm was definitely getting better. He hadn't felt it until he moved. She set the tray down and turned away.

"Where are you going?"

She looked down at him in surprise. "I was just going to give you some privacy."

"I'd rather you stayed here and talked to me," he said, patting the side of the bed.

Rather shyly she nodded and, gathering her skirt, she sat down on the edge of the bed.

"What are you going to do once I'm gone?" Quinn asked after taking a long swallow of a freshly made fruit juice.

"Wait for a ride back to Sirocco. Someone should be here in the next few days with a food shipment."

"Then what?"

She looked surprised. "Well, then I'll continue our work, of course."

"Of course," he murmured under his breath. "When do you intend to return to the States?"

"I agreed to stay here until the end of the year, then I'll go home and work with the group there, visiting campuses, giving speeches, encouraging more capable people to assist us in what we're doing."

"What about your personal life?" he asked, hating himself for prying.

She chuckled. "What personal life?"

"That's what I'm talking about. What are your long-range goals? Are you so determined to feed other people's children that you don't intend to have any of your own?"

There was no smile on her face now. "It isn't that I don't want a child. It's just that too many people today are working so hard to get ahead that they don't consider establishing a healthy family life a priority. I don't want to have a child that is shoved aside until the end of the day when we reach home, too tired to listen to him or her."

"Does it have to be that way?"

"I hope not. Except for the men who are currently working with this project, most of the men I know are like my brothers, working long hours to get ahead, determined to succeed at all costs."

"Are your brothers married?"

"Andy, the oldest one, but his wife is a lawyer, too. There's been no mention of having a family, which is just as well." She reached over and poured out the medicine for him to take and he just looked at her. Then, shaking his head with resignation, he opened his mouth. "What about you?"

He swallowed. "What about me what?"

"Haven't you wanted a family?"

Not until recently, he thought. "My situation is a little different."

"In what way?"

"You've seen the kind of life I lead. It isn't conducive to family harmony."

"Are you happy?"

He leaned back on the bed and looked at her. "I thought I was." He took her hand and brought her fingers to his mouth. He began to kiss each fingertip. He could feel her pulse racing under the thumb resting against her wrist. He was glad to know that he had some effect on her. She certainly created all sorts of reactions in him.

She sat their watching him without saying anything. Then slowly she touched his hair with her other hand. "I need to go and let you rest."

"All I've been doing is resting."

"But if you're still planning to leave—"

"I have no choice."

"Then stay here tonight, would you? Tomorrow is soon enough to return to your own world, isn't it?"

He sighed and closed his eyes. That damn medicine knocked him out. But he knew she was right. About most things, anyway. "Tomorrow is soon enough," he agreed, slowly opening his eyes to meet her gaze. He turned her hand so that he could kiss her palm. "Thank you."

"For what?"

"For talking to me. For being so honest with me. It means a lot to me, getting to know you."

Her voice sounded husky when she spoke. "It's meant a lot to me, too." She tried to smile. "Maybe you could write once in a while, let me know how you're doing?"

"Don't count on it. I'm not much for sending annual Christmas greetings."

As though reluctant to move, Jennifer slowly drew her hand away from him. Stroking his cheek, she whispered, "Rest now."

Quinn watched her walk out of the room and felt as though another knife had stabbed him in the gut, twisting and tearing until he wanted to cry out with the pain.

Determinedly he turned over on his side and closed his eyes. He might as well sleep. There sure as hell wasn't much else he could do.

A slight noise awakened him later and Quinn blinked open his eyes. It was night, and from the stillness all around him he guessed that it was fairly late. A small candle burned on a table by the grate, but there was no fire. A shadow on the wall made him realize that he wasn't alone and he raised his head.

Jennifer was moving around, arranging the pallet where she had been sleeping. As he watched, she pulled the kaftan over her head and folded it neatly before placing it on a nearby chair. She had no idea he was awake. He knew by her quiet, graceful movements that she thought she was unobserved.

She reached behind her and unclasped the wisp of material that covered her breasts, freeing them to his view. God! She was beautiful. Her small breasts were full and shapely, and her slender waist flared into gently rounded hips.

Quinn continued to watch as she reached for a sleeveless nightgown that skimmed her body and hung to the floor. The opaque material shielded her body from his view, but not from his memory. He had touched that body repeatedly in an effort to reduce her fever and had gotten to know it as though it were his own.

Jennifer sat down on the edge of a chair and began to pull her braid apart. He watched as she combed through it, causing her hair to cascade over her shoulders and down her back in flowing waves.

He sat up on the bed and she glanced up, startled, then smiled at him with her own very special smile, the one that caused such an ache somewhere in the region of his heart.

"How do you feel?" she whispered.

"Better. Is there a place I can bathe around here?"

She nodded and stood. Pulling the kaftan over her head once again, she glided past him and motioned for him to follow. He looked around for his clothes and found them near the bed. Instead of picking them up, he decided to wrap the sheet around himself and quickly followed her.

Once in the hallway, it was dark and she took his hand, quietly leading him to a door that she opened. She reached inside and turned on a light.

He was surprised at how functional the bathroom was. She smiled and without speaking closed the door behind him. There was a shower of sorts, and he gratefully stood under the water and soaped himself, keeping his left arm away from the spray. It was awkward working with one hand, and he knew that his arm was going to be a handicap for him. However, it might prove to be a blessing in disguise. Maybe he could convince Omar that he had been ambushed on his way back. He'd have to think about it, get a good story down.

By the time he was through, he felt refreshed and more like himself. Arranging his sheet around himself once more, he returned to the room he shared with Jennifer. She was waiting by the door.

"Did you have any trouble?" she asked softly.

"Not really."

"Let me check your dressing."

She motioned for him to sit down on the bed and she joined him. Jennifer quickly removed the bandages and looked at his arm. "How does it feel?"

"Better."

"It's looking pink and healthy. I'm pleased to see that it's knitting back together quite nicely." She covered it with a large patch and taped it securely. The new bandage was less bulky, Quinn noticed with relief.

She stood and had taken a step away from him when he took her hand and gently turned her around. She looked at him with a question in her eyes, but he didn't say anything, just continued to exert gentle pressure until she moved closer. Then he placed his hands at her waist and pulled her down on his lap.

Her eyes seemed to grow larger and darker in the flickering light from the candle, and the shadows in the room cast a cloak of intimacy around them. With infinite care Quinn lifted the hem of the kaftan until he could slip it over her head, then he tossed it on the floor.

"Jennifer?"

"Yes?" she responded almost inaudibly.

"There can never be anything between us, you know that, don't you?"

"Yes."

"But knowing that doesn't make it any easier for me to leave you."

Her eyes suddenly filled with tears, and she blinked as though to prevent them from spilling over. Her smile was so sad that it almost broke his heart. "Thank you for sharing that with me." As though she had no control over that part of her body, her hand reached out and stroked his cheek.

He felt a lump form in his throat. "I will never forget these past few days with you and the care you've given to me."

"You showed me the same care and consideration."

He slipped his arms around her and pulled her to him until her head rested on his shoulder. "I've never had to look after anyone before. I've always been alone, never needing anybody. Nobody has ever needed me before, either. It really felt strange to me at first, taking care of you. But there was no one else to do it. I couldn't let anyone else see that fair skin under your robes." He rocked her gently as though she were an infant.

"You've been very kind to me, much more patient than I deserved," she said softly.

He ran his hand slowly from the nape of her neck down her spine until it rested on her gently curving hips. She felt so good to him.

He shook his head. "Patience with you was the least of my worries. I was just trying to keep you alive."

"You did a good job," she pointed out, raising her head so that her lips brushed his cheek.

He inhaled sharply, then turned his head so that his lips were on the verge of touching hers.

Quinn didn't know which one of them moved that hairbreadth distance, but when he felt her lips touch his he could not resist. She greeted his kiss eagerly, opening her mouth, shyly greeting him with her tongue, playing with him, teasing him, imitating his bold strokes.

He could feel her trembling—or was that him? Her breathing was coming in little gasps, much like his. Quinn put his hands on either side of her head, lacing his fingers through the thick blond hair. He began to shower her face with kisses, as though he must touch each tiny place on her face—her eyes, her brows, her nose, her cheeks, that tender place in front of her ears.

Then, feeling as though he could no longer stand being away, he blindly searched for her mouth and sighed in satisfaction when he found it once more.

He knew this was insanity, knew that he had to stop. He had to stop now. And yet his hands continued to move, clutching her head, then sliding down her back around to the collar of her gown, where he brushed away the row of buttons as though they no longer existed. His hands parted her gown while he continued to kiss her, his mouth moving gently back and forth across hers, loving her, needing her, feeling her response with every fiber of his being.

Her gown now lay around her waist and his hands had the freedom to explore. He cupped her breasts in each of his hands, loving the slight weight of them, the way they seemed to grow in his hands, the way the tiny rose tips beaded into tight balls that called to him repeatedly for notice.

When he left her mouth and began a trail of kisses down her neck, Jennifer raised her head, silently giving him permission to continue. He slid one arm behind her so that she leaned against him, her breasts arched up to meet him.

He eagerly sought those siren tips that called to him so urgently. His mouth encircled one and his tongue flickered across it, back and forth...back and forth...and he felt her squirm against him. He allowed himself the pleasure of pulling slightly in a slow pulsating rhythm, pleased to hear her gasp and feel her quivering reaction.

Quinn moved his head until he found the other breast and lovingly repeated his actions. He held one breast while he gently stroked the other one, over and over, until he thought he was going to explode.

Jennifer's breathing was ragged when Quinn paused to take a breath. What were they doing? This was madness, utter and total madness. He wanted her so badly he ached with it, and he knew that he had aroused her to a point where she could no longer lie passively in his arms. Her restless shifting in his lap was creating havoc for him to the point that he was in actual pain. Only the thin material of her nightgown and his sheet separated her from his arousal.

"Jennifer? Jennifer, love?" he whispered.

She didn't open her eyes. Instead she turned her head so that her mouth was touching his shoulder. She began to place tiny kisses along his shoulder and toward his neck. Each place she touched set off a flaming torch that was searing his flesh.

"Hmm?"

"We have to stop this."

She didn't pause in her exploration. Her hand brushed across his chest until her fingertips touched the flat nipple hidden there. Then she bent her head and daintily flicked her tongue across his sensitive skin.

His body leaped as though he'd been electrocuted, but she didn't pull away. She mimicked his earlier actions with her, teasing, flicking her tongue back and forth until he groaned. Forcing her head up, he kissed her passionately, almost rough in his need for her, and she answered him wholeheartedly, her arms twining around his neck as though she had no intention of letting him go.

His heart was pounding so hard and so rapidly that it was jarring them both, so that even the bed on which they sat reverberated.

"Ah, love, forgive me, will you?" he finally muttered, lifting her off his lap and laying her down on the bed. With impatience he pulled her gown down with one swift tug until it cleared her feet. Then he tossed it aside to join her kaftan. His sheet had fallen away as soon as he stood, and he brushed it away. He stretched out beside her, his head resting on his hand.

"Forgive you for what?" she managed to whisper through kiss-swollen lips.

"For what I'm about to do. I've got to make love to you. I no longer have any choice."

"Yes," she agreed, reaching for him and pulling him down to her.

Seven

The striking contrast between his deeply tanned hand and her white skin fascinated him. He placed his hand on the satiny soft area of her abdomen just below her navel and felt the quiver that occurred beneath his palm.

Her arms encircled his neck, and he allowed her to pull his mouth down to hers. He edged his knee between her thighs and lay there, luxuriating in the intimacy of the moment.

"I don't want to hurt your arm," she whispered.

"I don't want to hurt you," he replied, kissing her on the ear.

"You won't." Her mouth grazed his cheek in a sliding nip.

"I can't protect you." His tongue touched her ear and she shivered.

"It doesn't matter." Her mouth searched for and found his.

He pulled away slightly. "It does to me."

"I mean, it's all right. I'm safe at the moment." Her gaze met his in the candlelight, clear and steady.

He shook his head. "Honey, you've never been safe with me, if you'd only known." He leaned down and encircled the tip of her breast with his lips.

She caught her breath and then sighed raggedly. "You know what I mean."

"Do you have any idea how badly I want you?" He tasted the other breast, tugging firmly, then letting it slide from his mouth.

"I want you, too. So much I ache with it," she whispered.

"Where do you ache, love?" He allowed his hand to slide lower. "Here?"

She nodded wordlessly as he kissed her once more, his tongue thrusting into her mouth as though he would show her how much he wanted to possess her.

"Or here?" he asked, his fingers riffling through the tight curls beneath his searching hand.

She unconsciously responded with a slight undulating movement of her hips, tilting upward toward his seeking fingers.

"Here, perhaps?" he whispered. He parted her fragile petal-shaped femininity and touched her.

"Yes!" she gasped, kissing him over and over wherever her lips touched his face.

Quinn had to force himself to concentrate on what he was doing or he would lose control completely. Never had he wanted a woman so badly in his life and yet this time…oh, my God! Yes! This time he wanted to give her so much pleasure, show her in every way he knew how what she meant to him. He wanted to worship her with his body, he wanted to share with her the experience of totally giving himself up to her for her satisfaction, which would give him his ultimate satisfaction, as well.

His finger lightly rubbed the sensitive spot he had found, so lightly he could scarcely feel her softness. Once again she made another undulating movement with her hips. Then he slipped his finger into her tight, moist warmth, darting in and out while his tongue imitated the same movement in her mouth.

She pulled her mouth away and sobbed. "Quinn! Oh, Quinn!" Her hands roamed restlessly across his back, then over his chest as though she didn't know where to touch him, what to do to respond, not knowing that her response was everything he could have hoped for, wished for, dreamed of. Her body was letting him know that she wanted him, that she was ready for him, and he knew that he couldn't hold off any longer.

Without removing his hand or changing his rhythm, he shifted his weight until both his knees were between hers, carefully nudging them apart.

Ah, she was so small, and he didn't want to hurt her. Never would he want to hurt this woman—this beautiful, most perfect woman.

He paused, his heart pounding so that he was shaking. He took a deep breath, then slowly slipped his hand from her. She groaned and lifted her hips to him.

"I know, little one, I know. I've started a raging fire inside you." He watched her face, the little frown between her brows, the hint of perspiration across her forehead, the way her tongue touched her lips, as though tasting him, tasting them together.

He was so hard and had been that way for so long that he hurt with it. He couldn't postpone gratification any longer, and yet there was so much more he wanted to do. So much pleasure he wanted to give her. But he couldn't wait. He had to have her. Now.

He moved over her, and she lifted to him so that he eased into her as though they had been designed to fit together. He could feel her tight warmth as he moved in short forward thrusts, taking his time until she could adjust to him.

She clutched at his shoulders, holding her breath as he allowed more of himself to enter.

Then he came to a barrier, and he stopped, stunned.

His eyes met hers. "Jennifer?"

"Please don't stop now," she pleaded, her breath coming in short pants.

"But, love, you—"

"Please, Quinn," she sobbed. "Oh, please."

He closed his eyes. My God. He'd never been faced with this situation before. Never in his life. No wonder she was so tight around him. No one had ever—

He had no choice. There was no going back now. With steady pressure he pushed and felt the tearing that seemed to be as much a part of his body as hers.

It was bad. He knew it was. She had covered her mouth with her hand and he'd heard her inarticulate, muffled scream. Just as he'd decided it wasn't worth it, nothing was worth hurting her like this, he was through the barrier and buried himself deep inside her.

Tears were pouring out of her eyes. All he could do was hold her close, kissing the tears as they rolled down her cheeks.

"I'm sorry, love. I'm so sorry. I never meant to hurt you. Oh, Jennifer, I never wanted to hurt you, love," he whispered in a hoarse voice.

She kissed him over and over and over on his lips, his cheeks, his nose, wherever she could touch him. "It's all right, Quinn. I knew it would hurt the first time. I just didn't know how much. But it doesn't matter." She paused and kissed him, her tongue touching him lightly, seeking his. "Don't you see, it really doesn't matter, not now."

As if to prove her point, she pressed her hips slightly upward, then moved them away from him, allowing them both to experience the wondrous sensation of his body so tightly embedded within hers, the sleek length of him caressing her in a newly sensitized part of her body.

Her generous and innocent movement was all it took to make him lose control completely. In his efforts to give her pleasure, he had inadvertently given

her pain. And yet, even in her pain and her innocence, she was seeking to give him pleasure.

Her generosity and courage swept him away.

Once started, Quinn could not contain the hunger
that drove him to move steadily, relentlessly, driven by
need that no man could resist. He could feel her tense
as his movements no doubt created new sensations
within her and he hoped, oh, how he hoped, that she
was able to feel the magic, the splendor, the awesome
wonder of this most intimate sharing.

He felt the sudden convulsive moment of rippling
muscle just as she cried out his name. Recognizing her
reaction for what it was, Quinn removed his own re-
straints and allowed himself to let go. The shattering
feeling that swept over him was indescribable as he
thrust faster and faster, feeling as though he were
being lifted higher and higher, wondering if he would
ever be the same again.

She was sobbing, her mouth pressed against his
throat. All he could think about was not crushing her
with his weight. He tried to shift, but she must have
thought he was trying to leave her and held on to him
tightly, her mouth touching him lightly in soft fluttery kisses.

He relaxed against her. "I'm too heavy for you," he
managed to say between gasps.

She just shook her head.

He rolled to his side away from his injured arm,
holding her locked against his body. Her body still
rippled with sensation, and he felt as though she were
stroking him over and over so that even while they lay

there trying to catch their breaths, he could feel himself growing hard once more.

Another first for him. He really must be dreaming.

He smoothed a strand of hair away from her face. "I hurt you," he said, so filled with regret he could hardly speak.

"No! You made me feel wonderful!" she responded fiercely. "I had no idea. None at all. What a beautiful experience."

"Yes. It was. I've never experienced anything even close to that before."

She opened her eyes and frowned. "Are you trying to make me believe that—"

He chuckled at her tone. "No. What I'm trying to say is that I've had sex before. This was the first time I've ever made love. I'm stunned."

She smiled, and he knew that her smile would haunt him for the rest of his life. "I'm glad. I feel pretty stunned, myself."

She gave a tentative wiggle and looked at him inquiringly. "I didn't know that it stayed that way."

"It never has before." Although he had experienced the relief of completion and felt the overwhelming relaxation of total release, Quinn realized that he wasn't ready to stop making love to her. "You must be sore," he offered quietly.

"I don't think so."

"Why didn't you tell me this was your first time?"

"I don't know. Somehow I could never find a way to work it into the conversation. Besides..."

"Besides, what?"

"I had no idea that you were interested in me."

"Not interested in you! Lady, you're even more innocent than I gave you credit for!"

"But you said earlier that we shouldn't—"

"And I meant it, but there was no way in hell I could let you go over there to your pallet and sleep tonight."

She kissed him. "I'm glad."

He rolled onto his back, pulling her with him, and her hair fell around them. "Our own special curtain of privacy. Just the two of us are here," he said, his mouth sliding over hers in a lazily possessive movement. "Have I told you how much I love your hair?"

She shook her head, making it shimmer and slither over their shoulders.

"Do you like horseback riding?" he asked with a slight smile.

"I don't have much time for it, but yes, when I can. Why?"

"Well, if you promise not to use a whip, I'll be glad to indulge you in the sport." Although he knew his voice sounded casual enough, he could feel the tension in his body. It was all he could do not to start moving deep within her. But this time he wanted her to feel that she was in control.

He coaxed her into an upright sitting position, then pulled her knees forward so that they rested alongside his hips. "Now, how's that?"

"You mean—"

He slipped his hands around her waist and lifted slightly, then allowed her to slide back down. He almost groaned aloud at the pleasurable sensation.

One thing he had to give her, Jennifer was a fast learner. She leaned forward slightly and began to rock against him. When he could no longer suppress his moan, she asked him anxiously, "Am I hurting you?"

His laugh caught in his chest. "That's not pain I'm feeling, love, believe me."

"Do you like this?" she said after a moment.

"Very much. How about you?"

She was silent, as though concentrating on the steady rhythm that had him clawing at the bed-clothes. "Yes. It's different, isn't it? The angle and everything."

"Yes," he managed to respond in a strangled voice.

"It makes me feel as though I'm in control," she said after a moment. She sounded as breathless as he felt.

"You are."

Perhaps he shouldn't have encouraged her, because she began to experiment with her movements, coming up on her knees so that she had more control, sliding oh-so-slowly down only to come up quickly, teasing him, provoking him, driving him out of his mind.

He could take no more.

He pulled her down to him and rolled until she was pinned beneath him. Playtime was over. His whole body felt as though he was going to jump out of it. He set a fast pace, and she instinctively lifted her legs and wrapped them around him, insuring that he couldn't leave her completely.

This time their release was simultaneous, her soft cry sounding in his ear as he gave in to the overwhelming sensation and let go.

Every muscle in his body was quivering in protest, and Quinn was suddenly reminded that he was recuperating from a gunshot wound. His arm ached abominably, and his body felt as though a herd of elephants had practiced the Mexican hat dance on top of him.

He lay there, collapsed on top of Jennifer, and began to laugh between trying to get some much needed oxygen into his lungs. He might die yet, but would this be considered complications of his wound?

Quinn managed to roll to his side, but his arms were too weak to hold her and Jennifer edged away from him, trying to see his face.

"What's wrong?"

"I think I'm trying to kill myself," he admitted, wiping the perspiration from his face with a corner of the sheet.

"Did I hurt your arm?"

"You didn't, love. I just forgot about the damned thing in the—uh—heat of the moment."

She sat up, looking around. "Maybe you should take some more medicine."

He reached for her, disgusted to see his arm tremble, his good arm at that. "I've got all the medicine I need, thank you very much. Just lie down, darling, will you?"

She stretched out beside him and placed her hand on his chest. His heart was thumping like a steam engine going up a steep grade. "Are you all right?"

"I will be, love. I just overexerted myself a little." He stroked his hand along her cheek and jawline. "I can't seem to get enough of you. The more you give, the more I want, and before I know it I can't move."

She smiled, enjoying the soft look in his eyes. The candle still flickered across the room, giving enough light for her to see him, to watch his expressions, and most importantly to look into his eyes.

Never had she seen eyes so black, as though the pupil had no ending. When she'd first seen him she had thought his eyes were hard and cold, but now that she knew him better she'd discovered they were the most expressive part about him. They could express so much emotion without his having said a word.

Now they seemed to be filled with light, as though his eyes and not the candle were illuminating the room. If she was ever to try to define love, she would have to find the words to describe the look in Quinn's eyes.

Neither of them had used the word, of course, as though it were taboo. For them, it was. They didn't need to talk about the fact that when he left in the morning they would never see each other again.

Jennifer tried not to think about tomorrow or the next day or the next. She didn't want to think about a whole lifetime that wouldn't have Quinn somewhere in it. She felt him moving and opened her eyes. He had gotten up and walked over to the table where the pitcher and water sat. He poured a glass of water and drank it, then poured some more water in a bowl, dipped one of the clean cloths in it and came back to the bed.

Kneeling down beside her, he brushed the damp cloth lightly against her. Despite everything they had just done, Jennifer felt herself flush. "What are you doing?"

"You must be sore, love. This will help." He bathed her gently, removing the evidence of her first time with a man. He went back to the bowl and rinsed the cloth, blew out the candle, then brought the freshly dampened cloth back to bed with him. This time he settled down beside her, turned her so that her back was to his chest and slipped his hand between her legs, holding the soothing cloth against her.

"Let's get some sleep, love. It's late."

She curled up beside him, loving the warmth of his body, enjoying the feel of his hair-roughened legs against the back of her thighs, knees and calves. She was touched by his consideration, because the cloth did help. He was right. She was sore. He had known she would be, and he was doing what he could to ease the pain.

How could she not love this man, she wondered, hearing his steady breathing and knowing that he had fallen asleep. A shiver of alarm went through her as she thought about his arm. It was healing so well. Hopefully they hadn't harmed it. She had tried to keep it in mind, but he had such a marvelous array of ways to distract her.

Jennifer was amazed that she hadn't felt the least bit shy with him. As much as she had tried to ignore the sexual tension between them since they met, she had recognized it for what it was, even though he'd given no indication that he had any intention of following up on it. What woman looking at him wouldn't have wondered what he would be like in bed? Just his walk indicated a sleek muscular control that she had only been able to guess at before tonight. Now she knew exactly how he used that beautifully honed body to please a woman.

Sleepily Jennifer wondered if there was any way Quinn could be convinced he would be an even greater asset to humanity if he continued to make love, and forgot about war.

Jennifer dreamed once again of being in a turquoise lagoon surrounded by white sands and swaying palms. Once again Quinn was there. Now there were no clothes to get in their way, and she eagerly threw her arms around his neck, wrapping her legs high around his waist in the chest-high water. She could feel him touching her in the secret place and it felt so good....

Jennifer opened her eyes, aware that part of her dream was more than a dream. In the dim light from the window, she discovered that she was stretched out on her back with her knees bent and open. Quinn was kneeling between her legs, kissing her.

"Quinn!" She tried to sit up, but he pressed his hand on her stomach and eased her back down.

"It's okay, love. I won't hurt you. I just want to love you, give you some pleasure."

"But you can't—I mean, you shouldn't—"

He looked at her, his eyes still full of light. "Don't you like this, love?"

His fingers were working their magic on her again. How could she not like it? "Yes, but—"

"Then just relax and enjoy it. I want you to get pleasure from me in every way I know to give it."

Relax, he said. How could she relax when his darting movements caused her body to respond in kind, lifting toward him, recognizing at long last what it had been missing all of these years.

Then he lowered his head and kissed her once again, and she let out a small cry. How had he known what that would do to her? His lightest touch seemed to galvanize her body to a point of stimulation where she thought she would shatter into a thousand pieces of pulsating feeling.

He held her gently but firmly as her body responded by flexing. She could feel the tension building inside her, even more intense than it had been earlier. It was as though a spring were being wound inside her, tighter, tighter and tighter until all at once, it was released, tossing her into another realm of sensation.

Jennifer pulled at his shoulders, urging him closer. "I don't want to hurt you, love. You've got to be sore."

All she knew was that she wanted him desperately, wanted him inside her. Wanted him now! Her hand brushed against him, and she felt the long smooth shaft that had shown her so much beauty and joy before. With a quick gasp she guided him to her, then lifted so that he slid inside.

"Oh, Jennifer," he gasped, no longer fighting her. She moved quickly, wanting to recapture the ecstasy again, feeling the tension immediately rebuild as his harsh breathing filled her ear. He was as affected as she was by her uninhibited response to his early-morning lovemaking.

Suddenly Jennifer felt as though she were exploding, the contractions of her sensitive muscles grabbing him until he, too, seemed to explode, holding her even tighter as they rode the shock waves together.

They fell asleep together this time, locked in each other's arms, as though daring fate to try to part them.

They were still entangled in each other's arms, their sheet lost to them hours before, when a tap sounded on the door and it opened.

"Jennifer! Haida said that—"

Jennifer opened her eyes just in time to see Paul's shocked face before he slammed the door.

Quinn stirred beside her and sleepily nuzzled her ear. "Who was that?" he murmured, and she remembered that he hadn't seen anyone of the household besides the doctor. Because she wasn't sure of the nature of what he was doing, she had felt it better to protect him as much as possible. He had no way of knowing the possible repercussions of Paul's coming in on them like that. She would have to deal with it, she knew, without involving Quinn.

"One of Haida's staff, I think," she lied.

She glanced down at them, visualizing what Paul must have seen, and she winced. There was no way that she could deny what had happened. But then, why should she try? She didn't owe anyone any explanations about the way she conducted herself, not even Paul.

But he might feel that you do, Jennifer reminded herself, and she silently acknowledged how much had changed in her life in just a few days. She had known Paul for four years. She had known Quinn for a week. She had finally allowed Paul a few lighthearted kisses. She had allowed Quinn—anything, and everything he wanted.

She didn't regret it. She would never regret these past few hours. Jennifer knew that she would never see him again. Even if they should run into each other here in Shiran, it would make no difference to the outcome of their relationship. They were each firmly following their own goals. Perhaps, ultimately, they were working for the same thing, but the paths they had chosen almost made them enemies at the moment.

Quinn had never opened his eyes. He had probably never come fully awake, but had accepted her calm explanation without question. She brushed her hand lightly across his back.

How could she ever treat Quinn as an enemy, even though she knew that Paul would see him entirely differently? If he knew that Quinn was with the same group that had shot him and captured her, he would do everything in his power to have him punished for it.

Yes. It was time for Quinn to leave, to go back to his guns, his fighting, his working toward his own version of peace. If he was in fact her enemy, she still found him irresistible.

"Quinn?"

"Hmm?"

"I think we need to get up."

He shifted, stretching, then winced when he moved his arm. "You're right. I've got to get on the road."

"Why don't you get dressed while I find something for you to eat. I've purposely kept you away from the rest of Haida's household. I wasn't sure you wanted anyone to see you and possibly recognize you."

He looked at her intently. "So you've been protecting me."

"Of course. You did the same for me."

"Even though you know I'm part of the group that captured you."

She leaned up on her elbow and ran her fingers lightly through his hair. "I know all I need to know about you, Quinn McNamara. Whatever your reasons for being in Shiran, they're your reasons, and I accept them."

"Even if you don't agree with them."

"Well, we're even. You don't agree with my reasons, either."

"That's for damned sure. It's too damned dangerous for you. And it's going to get worse."

She sat up and reached for her kaftan. "Is it?" she asked in a carefully neutral tone.

"Oh, hell," he said, coming off the bed and reaching for his pants. "Forget I said that." He stepped into them, then turned to her. "No. Remember I said it. Just don't ask any questions. Please, will you get the hell out of this country now? For me?"

"Does making love to me give you the right to tell me what to do?"

He shook his head and reached for his shirt. "Making love to you gives me no rights with you at all. I know that." He looked past her, but she saw the pain in his eyes. "Forget I said anything. We've got our own lives to lead. Let's get on with it." He searched in his shirt pocket and found his cigarettes.

She turned away and went to get him something to eat.

When she returned he had showered, his hair gleaming with droplets of water. Otherwise he looked the same.

"Thanks," he said quietly when she set the food down. He began to eat and started gathering some of the food in a cloth to take with him. Jennifer watched without saying anything.

When he finished he glanced around the room, then looked at her. "How do I get out of here?"

She walked to the door. "I'll show you."

Jennifer followed the hallway until she came to a connecting one, then turned. At the end of the second hall, she came to a door that was bolted. She slid the bolt and opened the door to an outside garden.

Staying in the shade along a high thick wall, she led him through the gardens to an overgrown path. The Jeep sat there with a tarp thrown over it.

"How did it get here?" he asked, removing the tarp and checking the Jeep over.

"I moved it. Haida said it would be safe here on the grounds. You can follow the trail about a hundred yards to the gate. Be sure to close and lock it behind you."

So. That was that. He had food, water, his Jeep. There was nothing to keep him from getting back to Omar.

He turned and looked at her, and the pain in his chest was so strong he thought he might be having a heart attack. Or perhaps that was the way a heart felt when it was breaking into small useless pieces.

She hadn't had time to put her hair in a braid. In fact, she didn't look as though she'd gotten much sleep. Her eyes were slightly puffy, as was her mouth, and there were mauve shadows beneath her eyes.

He slid his hand around to the nape of her neck. "Take care of yourself."

"I will." She seemed to be having trouble swallowing. "You take care."

"I always do."

She took a deep breath, as though trying to remember to breathe, then let it out slowly.

He leaned over and pressed his lips very softly against hers. "Thank you for coming into my life. I'll never forget you."

She nodded her head, but didn't speak. Her eyes glistened and she held them wide open, as though afraid to blink.

He turned away and got into the Jeep. It started on the first try. Without looking at her again, he backed up and turned around, carefully following the path to the gate.

Once through the gate, he got his bearings from the bright sun and headed south.

He'd been in that darkened room too long. The damned sunlight hurt his eyes, made them water. Impatiently he rubbed the back of his hand across his eyes, blinking to see the road in front of him, the road that took him away from Jennifer Sheridan.

Eight

Washington, D.C., in the springtime was a sight to behold, Quinn decided. He hadn't been here in three years and he was feeling a little out of place.

He glanced down at his air force uniform, still surprised to see the insignia of his latest promotion on his collar. Funny how things work out. It seemed that everything he did that last year in Shiran was wrong, everything went to hell, and he ended up getting a promotion out of it.

Max reminded him that there was no reason for him to be modest about his accomplishments and advised him to accept his commendation and promotion with graceful humility. The humility was easy enough to come by. He wasn't sure about the rest of it.

He paused, looking around him at the number of couples strolling along the way, enjoying the cherry blossoms, the warm spring day, and each other.

He reached into his pocket, pulled out a roll of mints and absently stuck one in his mouth. He wondered if Jennifer ever walked along here with someone, enjoying the beauty, the serenity. He hoped so. She would enjoy it.

Jennifer was so much a part of him that he didn't find it strange to be thinking about her. He thought about her all the time, not as he'd last seen her that morning over a year ago, watching him gravely as he told her goodbye. No, whenever he thought of Jennifer, he saw her smiling the special smile that seemed to light up her face. And he always saw her eyes. They were smiling, too, of course, so clear and so open to him.

He hoped that she was happy. He wanted her to have found everything in life that she wanted. He began to walk again, his thoughts back in Shiran.

He remembered returning to the village where he'd spent his time in Shiran. Omar had been glad to see him and had asked very few questions. He had been too busy plotting to take over the country to be concerned about one of his men straying for a few days with a beautiful woman. The only thing he had asked was whether Quinn had taken care of the problem.

That was one way of putting it, he supposed. He had taken care of the hostage problem so as not to create any trouble with the United States, but he had created a few problems for himself.

The takeover had been rough, just as Quinn had been afraid it would be. By the time they moved north to Sirocco, the government in power realized what was happening. It was too late to prevent Omar's takeover, but there was a good deal of resistance and a great many lives were lost.

Quinn watched and reported to Max and tried to keep himself from getting killed. And he kept remembering Jennifer's remark about killing for peace. Well, in her case he hadn't proved to be much of a proponent for chastity, either, as far as that goes.

It was only when Omar had taken charge of the country that Quinn had tried to see how the Feed the Children people had survived. Until then, it would have been too dangerous for them to have him hanging around. In the back of his mind he had hoped to find Jennifer, to make sure she was all right. But when he found the headquarters, he discovered that it was being run by natives of Shiran, who were efficiently seeing that the shiploads of food were being distributed. No one there had ever heard of Jennifer Sheridan.

Right after that, Omar had summoned him. He hadn't seen much of Omar after the takeover, for obvious reasons. The man was trying to set up a new government and deal with those in the old regime who didn't believe that he was there to save the country.

Quinn would never forget that day.

Quinn knocked on one of the double doors that led to Omar's office. Two guards stood on either side, staring straight ahead. This was a far cry from the small back room they used to meet in.

"Come in."

Quinn opened the door to a massive office with marble floors and fluted columns. Omar stood up when he saw Quinn and came around a desk that looked as big as a basketball court.

"Ah, Rashid. It's good to see you again. It's been a while, hasn't it?"

"You've been busy."

"Yes, and so have you. I wanted you to know that I'm aware of how many loose ends you tied up for me. You have been a great help to me during this time, and I wanted to discuss how I might repay you."

Ah, yes. Political favors time. It didn't much matter what he offered. Quinn knew that he would be in Shiran only until Max told him he was no longer needed there. Then he'd be sent to some other hot spot in the world. He wondered why they couldn't plan a revolution in the Antarctic sometime. It would make a nice change of scenery.

"I believe it is time for us to lay our cards out on the table, don't you?" Omar asked, smiling and motioning to Quinn to take a seat.

"I suppose. What sort of cards are we showing?"

"It served my purposes for you to work with me as Rashid Quoram, Major McNamara. Now we no longer need the charade."

Quinn sat perfectly still, trying to deal with the shock that Omar had just handed him.

"You are perhaps surprised that I was aware of your identity, Major."

"A little, yes." Never had Quinn wanted a cigarette so badly. He reached into his pocket and absently searched for his mints.

Omar walked behind the desk once more and sat down. He leaned back and placed his feet on the desk and his hands behind his head.

"It served my purpose, having you with me, of course."

"In what way?"

"I wanted your country to know exactly what I was planning and why. I intended to use that communication source if I needed help pulling off the coup, you see."

"You never asked."

Omar shrugged. "No, because with your excellent advice on strategy, I was always able to utilize the men and positions I had. I didn't trust you at first, of course, because I didn't understand your motives. At that time I merely wanted you where I could keep an eye on you. It was only later that I realized you were truly behind the takeover."

"I wasn't, not at first."

"What changed your mind?"

"The way you handled the hostage situation."

Omar grinned. "Ah, yes. Jennifer Sheridan."

"Did you know who I was when she was captured?"

"But, of course. Why do you suppose I turned her over to you so promptly? I was greatly angered by those bungling fools. I was afraid their impulsive actions would destroy everything I had set out to achieve. Luckily, you were there and I could let you deal with the rather delicate matter.''

So all the time Quinn had thought he was being a hotshot, convincing the natives that he was Rashid Quoram, Omar had been fully aware of who he was and had used him.

''Why didn't you say something back then?''

''Why should I? You handled the matter. I always assumed you took her back to Sirocco.''

''Close enough.''

''Where you really shot by bandits?''

''That part was true.''

''You came back and seemed to double your efforts to help me.''

''Believe it or not, I wasn't as interested in helping you as it might appear. What I was trying to do was to avert bloodshed in the country. Unfortunately, I didn't succeed very well.''

Omar looked at him in surprise. ''But there is always a certain amount of loss of life in situations such as these. That is unfortunate, regrettable even, but unavoidable.''

''But it's always done in the name of peace.''

''Yes, of course! That is what we are all here working for. I know that. You know that. And we have come a long way.''

''I wonder if that makes a difference to the grieving mothers and widows of the men who didn't live through the coup.''

"But we have provided a more stable place from which they can raise their children."

"Have we? Until the next would-be savior comes along, I suppose."

Omar looked puzzled. "I'm afraid I don't understand you."

"I know. I'm not sure that I understand myself these days. Maybe I've been over here too long."

"But that is what I wanted to discuss with you. I am pleased with our relationship with your country. I would like to place you in a position of authority here, in the hope that we will continue to cooperate with one another, both on a one-to-one level as friends, and also country to country."

"Yes, I can see where such an alliance would be beneficial to you, Omar."

"And to your country, as well, don't forget. I am certain that they would rest easier knowing that the plentiful supply of oil we have here would be readily available should the United States have need of it."

Quinn leaned forward. "You've certainly given me a great deal to think about, Omar. I'll have to contact the man I report to and let him know that our charade here in Shiran was a farce."

"No, no. Never that. You were quite good, as a matter of fact. It's just that I have a very efficient intelligence group of my own."

Quinn shook his head. He was too old for this game. He could have gotten himself killed. In fact, it was a wonder he hadn't been eliminated.

* * *

Quinn stopped walking and looked up, recognizing his hotel. He turned in and walked over to pick up his key. He was given a message to call Max.

Good old Max. He had agreed that there was no longer any reason for Quinn to stay in Shiran once Omar revealed his knowledge. Instead Shiran now had an official U.S. adviser and an office down the hall from the double-doored office.

And Quinn had come home, feeling like a fool, dissatisfied with life and missing Jennifer as though he'd had a limb severed.

He'd been kicking around D.C. for ten days now, waiting for a new assignment, trying to work up enough courage to get in touch with Jennifer.

As soon as he got to his room, he returned Max's call.

"Do you have any plans for tonight?" Max asked as soon as Quinn identified himself.

"Nothing that can't be altered. Do you need me for something?"

"Well, there's some kind of social function going on, and we've been asked to furnish some people to keep an eye on things. I thought if you were bored enough it might interest you. Good food and drinks, some dancing, that sort of thing."

"Am I supposed to go disguised as a waiter or something?"

Max laughed. "No, you go disguised as Lieutenant Colonel Quinn Lewis McNamara, USAF."

"Wow, that would be different, chief. I'll probably forget to answer to my own name." Jennifer popped into his mind, and he could hear her chanting his name breathlessly as he made love to her. "Sure, why not? As you say, I don't have anything better to do."

Max gave him the details, including address and time, and Quinn hung up. He glanced at his watch. He had time to take a nap before getting ready.

He was tired. Inaction always made him tired. Maybe a few hours of music and a lavish spread of food would change his mood.

Although the prestigious hotel had a large ballroom, the size of the crowd seemed to dwarf it. From an alcove overlooking the dance floor, Quinn watched the colorful parade and listened to the babble of voices. He was totally out of place here and he knew it.

He sipped on his second drink of the evening. He'd already polished off a plate of expensive delicacies. Now he was earning his keep by watching people.

Quinn wondered if he had a niche in life at all. He no longer cared about what he was doing in the air force and had asked to be transferred to another area. Of course he could always retire. He'd been in the service more than long enough for that. But then what? What would he do? Where would he go?

He didn't care for gatherings like this, he wasn't good at social repartee. Being able to interrogate a hostile prisoner efficiently didn't count in these surroundings.

His gaze drifted to a tall white-haired man on the dance floor. He moved with a grace that spoke of another era of ballroom dancing. Quinn smiled and watched as the man swung around to face him, then he lowered his glass and stared at the familiar face. Not that he'd ever met him in person, but he recognized the man. It was Senator Andrew Sheridan.

Quinn grasped the railing and hung on, surprised to find himself weak at the knees. Why the hell was he surprised to see Senator Sheridan? The place was crawling with senators and representatives.

Quinn looked at the woman dancing with the senator. She was short and rather plump, with carefully coifed hair. Was that his wife? Jennifer had never mentioned her mother, and he had assumed that she was dead. But he didn't know. He forgot to watch anything else for the rest of the dance. Here was a way he could find out something about Jennifer, if he had the courage. He could casually introduce himself, mention that he and Jennifer had met in Shiran, and ask about her. If he dared.

Quinn could feel his heart speed up and his adrenaline start pumping just at the thought. Normally he didn't have that much of a reaction when he was going into combat, for crying out loud.

He watched to see where the couple went when the dance was over and saw them move to a large circular table. Perhaps he'd go down there, and if there was an opportunity, he might decide to say something to them.

Then again, he might not. After all, what difference did it really make? But then, he would feel better knowing she was well. He found the stairway and went down to the ballroom.

In an effort to get his bearings, he glanced up to where he'd been standing, then sighted over to where the table appeared to be and began to move—

"Oh, excuse me, I—" a laughing voice was saying.

He looked down and saw that he had just run into Jennifer. He stared at her hungrily, looking for changes. She had her hair done up in some sophisticated style that left her ears free to display a dazzling pair of diamond earrings. Matching diamonds were around her neck. The white satin dress she wore was strapless, revealing a hint of a shadow between her breasts. The skirt was slim, faithfully following the contours of her hips and thighs.

She looked wonderful, and she was staring at him in confusion. She glanced at his uniform, then back to his clean-shaven face.

"Don't I—" Her face went very white and she swayed. He reached out and steadied her. "Quinn?" she murmured as though to herself. "Is it you?"

Well, you wanted to know how she was doing, now's your chance to say something, he reminded himself.

"Hello, Jennifer." Now that was impressive. That shows some really inventive, profound thought.

She began to smile, the color rushed back into her cheeks and she said, "You shaved your beard! I almost didn't recognize you. And I was right! You do have dimples. I thought you did."

Dimples? Without thinking, he touched his cheek with his fingertips, feeling totally out of his depth.

"When did you get back? How long are you here? Oh, wait until I introduce you to Dad. I told him all about meeting you and how you saved my life and—" She paused and looked at him, puzzled. "Quinn?"

He took her hand. "You told your dad about us?"

She shook her head quickly. "Well, not everything, of course, although I'm sure he suspects that—"

"That what?"

She shrugged. "That I met someone in Shiran who stole my heart."

"And did you?"

She glanced up at him from beneath her lashes. "And what do you think, Colonel McNamara?"

He stared down at her in amazement. He couldn't take in all that was happening to him at the moment. Without smiling, he said, "I think you're flirting with me."

Her smile faded. "I'm just glad to see you, Quinn. That's all." She glanced over her shoulder. "May I introduce you to my parents?"

He nodded and allowed her to lead him over to the table he'd been watching earlier. He could think of many things he'd rather do than meet her parents under these conditions. What the hell had she told them about him? He seemed to have lost all control over the situation.

"Dad! You're never going to believe who I just ran into. Do you remember my speaking of Quinn Mc-

Namara, who was doing some kind of hush-hush work over in Shiran when I was there? Well, I've just discovered that he is now Lieutenant Colonel Quinn McNamara." She turned to Quinn with the smile that had kept him company every day and night for the past year. "Quinn, I would like to introduce my father, Andrew, and my mother, Marian."

Senator Sheridan came to his feet, and Quinn discovered where Jennifer had gotten her smile. "Well, Colonel, this is certainly a pleasure. Jennifer has told us how you saved her life last year. I can't begin to express the debt of gratitude we feel."

God, he hated this. He hated standing there nodding and smiling to a man whose daughter he had seduced. How could Jennifer look so relaxed and happy? But then, perhaps she had already forgotten who the first man had been. Maybe there had been so many others since then that—

Stop it! You know better. She would not give herself lightly to anyone, and if she's found someone else, that's what you've been hoping for, isn't it? You've wanted her happy, haven't you?

"Sit down and join us, Colonel," the senator was saying, motioning to a chair.

Jennifer must have caught the expression on Quinn's face, because she began to speak.

"If you'll excuse us, Dad, Mom, but I just this minute ran into him and there's so much news to catch up on. Would you excuse us? I'm sure you'll see more of him later," she added.

As they made their way through the tables, Quinn muttered, "Thanks for getting me out of that one."

She glanced over her shoulder. "I recognized that look on your face and knew that it boded ill to anyone who made you sit down and attempt to be polite!"

He began to laugh. "That bad, huh?"

"You haven't really changed that much." She studied his face. "I kinda miss the beard, though. However, you are a very handsome man, Colonel McNamara, with or without a beard."

He found himself grinning. "Cut out the 'colonel' and we'll still be friends."

The music started up and Jennifer said, "Would you like to dance?"

"I'm not very good on a dance floor."

"That's okay. Neither am I."

She led the way out onto the floor, turned and lifted her hands.

So for just a little while he was going to have her in his arms again. Not a bad trade-off, all things being equal. It was almost worth having to meet her parents.

Jennifer kept studying his face. "Without your beard, you don't look Shiranese at all. You look very American. Of course," she pointed out, "wearing an American military uniform helps."

"Thanks," he responded in a wry voice.

"Don't mention it," she said, resting her head on his shoulder.

His body was signaling all sorts of urgent messages to him, reminding him that it had been a year since he'd made love to a woman, and now that very woman was in his arms, dancing seductively close to him.

The same floral scent tormented him, and he was aware once again of how well they fit together. There was no way she could not be aware of the effect she was having on him. Damn her, anyway.

She looked up at him and that clear-eyed gaze went right through him. "Are you here tonight by yourself, Quinn? I never thought to ask."

"Yes. How about you?"

"I came with my folks, but I don't have to leave with them."

"Meaning?"

"That if you'd like to be a gentleman and offer to take me home, I'd accept."

He laughed at her demure tone of voice. "I'm afraid it wouldn't be my gentlemanly instincts that would cause me to offer to take you home, Jennifer."

"Does that mean you aren't offering?"

"That means you will be much safer going home with your parents."

"Oh."

They danced for a few minutes in silence. Quinn realized that he was gathering more memories to go with the ones he already had.

"Quinn?"

"Hmm?"

"What are you doing in Washington?"

"I'm being reassigned."

"You finished whatever you were doing in Shiran?"

"Yes."

"I worried about you during all the fighting."

"I worried about you, as well. I had no way of contacting your organization without endangering you and them. Then by the time we got to Sirocco, no one there knew anything about you."

"But you looked for me?" she asked in pleased surprise.

He looked down at her in irritation. "Don't sound so damned surprised. Of course I looked for you. I told you I would."

"Well, you'll be pleased to know that I took your advice."

"About what?"

"About returning to the States. I left a few weeks after I last saw you."

Now that did surprise him. He stopped dancing, only to have someone behind them run into them. "Sorry," he said over his shoulder and began moving again. "Why?"

"Because of what you wouldn't tell me. I knew you were worried, and I knew you were working with a guerilla group that was keeping a low profile at the time. I decided you were trying to warn me about something."

"Well, I'll be damned. I can't believe you really listened to me." He swung her around in a fancy step that had her laughing.

"I thought you said you can't dance!"

"Not very well."

"Then you must have been watching a bunch of Fred Astaire movies."

He grinned at her, enjoying her flushed cheeks and bright eyes. She was evidently pleased to see him and didn't care if he knew it. Did she have any idea how much better that made him feel about everything that had happened between them? He had tried to convince himself that he had not taken advantage of the situation, that theirs had been a mutual decision, that she had known what she was doing.

But he didn't always win that argument with himself.

Now to see her laughing up at him, flirting with him, made him feel as though he hadn't done any permanent harm.

He cleared his throat. "Uh, as long as we're confessing, I took your advice, as well."

"About what?"

"I gave up smoking."

"You? I don't believe it!"

"I got to thinking about what you said. When I was unconscious I gave my body a few days without them. I decided to see how long I could put off smoking one. Every time I'd put one in my mouth, I'd suddenly see you in my mind, pointing out all the perils."

"Well, it's good to know you thought of me once in a while."

He found that he couldn't find a lighthearted response, so he said nothing.

The music stopped and they paused, looking at each other. The dance was over, and he knew it was time for him to turn around and walk out of her life. He knew she was well, obviously happy, what more did he need to know?

He heard himself ask, "Are you still working with the Feed the Children project?"

She nodded, walking off the floor. "Yes. As a matter of fact, we've been negotiating with a South American nation for permission to go into the country and set up some way stations for feeding some of the people whose crops have been destroyed by the recent drought."

So her life was still set on its path, just as his was. Hopefully they wouldn't be in the same country at the same time, because that would mean she'd picked a country filled with strife.

"Well, Jennifer, it's been good to—" he began, only to be interrupted.

"Quinn? What if I don't want to be safe?"

"I beg your pardon?" Had she turned into some sort of mind reader?

"You said earlier that I'd be safer if I allowed my parents to take me home, remember?"

"I remember."

"Well, what if I don't want to be safe?"

"You want me to take you home, I gather."

"Very much."

"Jennifer, I—"

"Please don't turn me down, Quinn. It's just that we haven't seen each other in so long. And there's so much I want to find out. What you were doing in Shiran, if you can tell me now, how the coup worked."

She looked away, unable to meet his eyes. "There's just so much I want to know," she said softly, her voice dwindling away.

Come on, McNamara, surely you can behave yourself for a few short hours. Just make sure you aren't near any beds and for God's sake make sure you both keep your clothes on. After all, you're a civilized person. You've learned self-control.

"All right, Jennifer. When do you want to go?"

Her smile almost blinded him with its brilliance. "I'm ready now if you are."

If she had any idea just how ready he was, she would never have suggested that he take her home!

Nine

After Quinn had contacted the officer in charge of security to let him know he was leaving, they took a cab to her home. Quinn discovered that it was on a quiet street of older apartment complexes. A doorman greeted them, and they went upstairs in a rather slow, halting elevator.

"Has that thing ever stopped between floors?"

"Not that I know of," she said when they stepped off. "But it definitely has a personality all its own."

"Have you lived here long?" he asked, looking around the hallway while she searched for her key.

"Eight years. I moved here after I graduated from college."

"Do you live alone?" He heard himself sounding like twenty questions, but damn it, he was curious. Obviously she didn't live with a man, unless they had a very open relationship.

She laughed. "Oh, no. Dad wouldn't hear of his only daughter moving into an apartment alone. So he insisted that Mandy come live with me."

"Mandy?"

"She's worked for us ever since I started school." She finally found her key and opened the door. A tall black woman came down the hallway. "Mandy, I want you to meet Colonel Quinn McNamara, a friend of mine I haven't seen in a while. We're going to have some coffee, but you don't need to stay up."

"I'm pleased to meet you, Colonel," Mandy said with a warm smile.

"Quinn, why don't you go on into the living room. I'm going to get out of these shoes and find something more comfortable to wear. I'll be back in a minute."

He wandered into the living room while Mandy and Jennifer disappeared down the hallway.

That's exactly what he was afraid of. He didn't want her getting into anything more comfortable. If she walked into the room wearing the kaftan he'd last seen her in, he'd be done for.

So why are you fighting it, anyway? he wondered. You're both adults. What's wrong with indulging in some pleasurable hours, keeping in touch, and when you both happen to be in D.C. at the same time, you get together?

Because he couldn't do that, that's why! Leaving her was the hardest thing he had ever had to do in his life. He couldn't do it again, not if he made love to her. Obviously there were men who could have affairs and not get emotionally involved. Hell, he'd had a few himself. But not this time. Jennifer had carved a niche for herself in his heart, and she would always be there. It was almost easier not seeing her at all than getting glimpses of her here and there. It would never be enough.

"Why don't you take off your jacket and tie and get comfortable?" Jennifer walked into the room wearing a pair of multi-washed jeans and a sweatshirt with a faded university emblem on it. The earrings and necklace were gone, and she was rapidly pulling down her hair.

He felt like a fool, standing there afraid to remove even the most innocuous of wearing apparel. It was obvious that Jennifer wasn't trying to be seductive. She probably had no idea what the jeans did to him. He followed her suggestion while she went on into the kitchen and started the coffee. When she came back, she was combing out her hair. It was still long, but not as long as it had been in Shiran.

"I don't know why I allow myself to be talked into going to those things. I can't stand them." She looked at him and smiled, obviously pleased to see him sitting there on her sofa. "You comfortable enough?"

"I'm fine. Thanks."

"So what were you doing there? You don't strike me as a person who would enjoy those kinds of gatherings."

"I don't. I was there out of duty more than pleasure."

"I know what you mean," she commiserated. "I can only say no so many times before I get engineered into going. I'm glad I did, though. Otherwise I wouldn't have gotten to see you."

"I was planning to call you," he heard himself saying.

"Oh, were you? When?"

When I got up enough courage, he was tempted to say. "Well, I wasn't sure where to reach you."

"I'm in the phone book."

"Oh."

Jennifer excused herself and went in to get their coffee. In a few minutes she brought it out on a tray, and he was once again reminded of her looking after him, bringing him food on a tray, giving him medicine.

"I'm surprised you don't hate me," he blurted out.

She glanced up in surprise. "Why do you say that?"

"Because of everything that happened between us."

"Do you mean because we made love together?"

Well, hell, lady, why don't you be blunt and just say what you mean?

He picked up his coffee and took a sip. She made great coffee. "Yes," he finally said. "I suppose that's what I mean."

She took a sip of her coffee, then set it down. "Quinn, I don't want you to feel awkward with me, or embarrassed. I did what I did because I wanted to, not because you forced me in any way. And it was the most beautiful experience of my life. Never once, not once, have I ever regretted making love with you."

Her husky voice caught at him, pulled at him so that he was hard put to hide the emotion she evoked.

"Have you ever thought about leaving the air force?" she asked, picking up her cup again.

He shifted slightly at the change of subject, but perhaps it was just as well. "More than once," he admitted wryly, thinking back over the past few months.

"What would you do if you retired?"

He shrugged. "That's what has kept me doing what I've been doing. It's the only thing I'm trained for. It's the only thing I know."

"Have you ever thought about putting some of your special knowledge to work in another area?"

He looked at her blankly.

She leaned forward slightly. "I mean, would you consider going to work for us?"

He looked at her warily. "I'm not sure I understand. Who is 'us'?"

"The Feed the Children program." As though she could no longer sit still, she stood and began to pace the room. Quinn couldn't keep his mind off how well those jeans fit her shapely legs. And he remembered her legs so well.

He forced his attention to what she was saying, surprised when he heard, "I've given a great deal of

thought to the things you said to me when we were together, and you were right in many ways. I mean, we
really are a bunch of idealists that got together to try
to do something that would make a difference in this
world, but sometimes we aren't too practical. Being in
Shiran at that time was a good example. It was a little
too easy to get caught up in the zeal of the moment
and become martyrs, but in the long run, I had to face
the fact that we were not going to accomplish our pri-
mary purpose by martyring ourselves.''

Quinn nodded. "I'm not sure what that has to do
with me. I'm afraid I'm not martyr material, myself."

She stopped pacing and looked at him from across
the room. Her hands were gripped together tightly, the
only sign she showed of her tension. "We need someone on the Executive Board who would keep our feet
on the ground. You have contacts. You know what's
going on in the world. Maybe you'd want to do some
fieldwork from time to time. You wouldn't get rich on
what we'd be able to pay, but then, none of us do."

Quinn could feel the spurt of excitement hit him,
and he tried to keep a tight rein on his emotions. "So
we would be working together?" he asked cautiously.

She grinned, the impish grin that he always found
so delightful. "I was afraid you'd catch that right off.
Yes, there is an ulterior motive. I'd get to spend more
time with you."

He suddenly noticed that his cup was rattling in his
saucer. He carefully put both of them down. "And
that would please you?"

Her gaze never left his. "More than anything in the world," she said softly.

Quinn was having trouble breathing. He stood and took a couple of steps toward her and stopped, afraid to think that there was a chance for the two of them. "Jennifer—"

"Yes?"

She was watching him so carefully. He could feel her tension mount. Or was it his? He took the necessary steps to cover the space between them and grabbed her, pulling her into his arms and holding her too tight. He knew she wouldn't be able to breathe, but he needed to hold her so damn much. Forcing himself to relax his arms, he buried his head in her hair.

"God, Jennifer! I missed you so much. So damned much. I thought I was going to die from it," he whispered, his voice choked.

Her arms were wrapped tightly around his waist. "I missed you, too, Quinn. You'll never know. I was so afraid you'd been killed, and I didn't know who to contact here in the States, and I was afraid to ask questions in Shiran—"

His mouth cut her off. Quinn tried to show her without words what he felt for her, how much he'd missed her and how lonely he'd been.

Without releasing her mouth, he scooped her into his arms and strode to the sofa. He leaned back along its length, holding her to him, never wanting to let her go. He could no longer think or plan. The future was some nebulous place that he cared nothing about, if he could just have this moment.

He became aware that Jennifer's fingers were working at the buttons of his shirt, and he drew away slightly. "Oh, love, be careful. You don't know what you're asking for."

"Oh, but I do! I want you to hold me, and love me, and I want to love you. I want to know if my memories have made more of what we had, because nothing could possibly be as earthshakingly beautiful as what I remember." She had his shirt open and began to plant kisses on his throat, rubbing her hand across his chest as though relearning his body.

He felt a shudder run through him at her touch. He knew exactly what she was saying, because he'd wondered the same thing. The mind could play funny tricks on a person.

Suddenly she sat up away from him. He opened his eyes. She stood and held out her hand. He glanced around the room and knew that unless he intended to walk out the door right that minute, he was going to follow her.

He knew that he wasn't leaving.

Quinn stood and took her hand and was rewarded with one of her illuminating smiles. She led him to the foyer, pausing only long enough to turn off the lights. Putting her finger to her lips, she followed the hallway to the door at the end, opened it and stood back for him to enter. He walked into a large plushly furnished bedroom with a small lamp burning beside the bed.

"Looks considerably different from what I'm used to," Quinn said. His voice sounded hoarse.

She walked over to him and hugged him without saying a word.

Did she have any idea what he was feeling? he wondered. He'd never been in a situation like this before. He was making a commitment to someone, he was offering to become a part of her life in whatever way she would accept him.

Quinn felt as though he had just taken a wild leap into a black void. He had no idea where he was headed or how he would land.

At the moment, though, having Jennifer in his arms was all the security he needed.

He slid his hands under her sweatshirt and discovered that she wasn't wearing a bra. His hands cupped her breasts as though that's where they belonged. But he couldn't see them, and he lifted the sweatshirt over her head and tossed it aside. He leaned down and touched first one, then the other, with his mouth.

She shivered and whispered, "Quinn?"

"Mmm?"

"I don't think my knees are going to hold me up much longer," she admitted shakily.

He could certainly relate to the feeling. He sat down on the edge of the bed, his shirt open to the waist, and pulled her to him. He unfastened her jeans with trembling hands and slid them down her legs. Quinn couldn't resist pressing his mouth against her, and he heard her slight whimper.

He pulled her down beside him, and she feverishly tugged at his belt. With a grin he stood and pulled off his slacks, managed to fold them and drape them across a chair. He quickly removed the remainder of his clothing while she lay there watching him with shining eyes.

"I never thought I'd ever see you here in my bedroom," she admitted.

He stretched out beside her. "I never expected to be here."

She leaned over him, running her hands down his body. He could feel his muscles quivering. When she reached his hardened length, he clamped down on his lip to keep from groaning aloud. It had been so long. So very long.

"I've lain awake nights thinking of all the things I would like to have done with you," she whispered, her hair brushing against his chest.

"I know the feeling."

She smiled, then slowly lowered her head to his stomach. Her hair formed a veil between them, so that when her lips touched him intimately he was unprepared.

"Jennifer!"

Her only response was to continue to love him until he thought he would go out of his mind. When he could no longer endure the pleasure that she was giving him, he drew her up over his body and eased himself carefully inside her.

Quickly she began to move as though afraid he would try to take control. There was no need for her to worry. Quinn was too enthralled in all the sensations she was creating to do more than respond to her. And when she gave a small cry and sprawled across his chest, her body convulsing around him, he felt as though his whole body exploded like fireworks on the Fourth of July, shattering into bits of light and color, then slowly falling back to earth.

They lay there together while Quinn lazily ran his hand over her head, his fingers playing with her hair. For the first time in a year, he felt at peace—with himself and with the world.

"Do you have any idea how much I love you?" he finally said, his voice sounding a little ragged.

She raised her head and looked at him. "Do you, Quinn?"

"More than I've ever loved anyone in my life. So much that it frightens me."

"Why should it frighten you?"

"Because I don't know what to do with these feelings. Sometimes I feel almost overwhelmed by them."

"Would it help you to know that I feel the same way about you?"

He shifted so that they lay side by side, their legs still entangled. "I find that so hard to believe."

"I don't know why. You're very lovable, you know."

He just shook his head.

She kissed him on his chin. "You have a lovely jawline, did you know that? Very strong." She touched his chin. "With just a hint of a cleft." Her fingers traced the lines by his mouth and she smiled. "And dimples."

He grinned. "What's all this about dimples?"

"I've always loved them, but no one in my family has them."

"We need to talk about that."

She leaned up on her elbow and stared down at him with slightly raised eyebrows. "Dimples?"

"No. Your family."

"Oh." She tucked her head under his chin. "What about them?"

"What are they going to think about your marrying me?" There. He'd finally said the words. He knew that she could feel his heart pounding directly beneath her ear. Maybe she would assume it was because of their recent lovemaking.

"Do you want to marry me?" she whispered.

He wished he could see her face. "I don't know anything about being married—" he began.

"That wasn't what I asked you."

"I just want you to be a part of my life, in whatever way we can work out."

She was quiet for so long that he decided she must have fallen asleep.

Well, what did you think? That she'd be overjoyed with your matchless performance, your magnificent offer? He closed his eyes and tried not to think.

"My family would accept anyone I wanted to marry," she finally said. "I've been on my own for some time now. They respect my judgment and accept me as my own person."

He could find no response to that.

"Do you truly want to marry me, Quinn?" she said after a few moments, lifting her head and meeting his gaze.

"More than I've ever wanted anything."

Her gaze still locked with his, she nodded. "Yes, Quinn. I would be honored to marry you and be your wife. Nothing would give me more pleasure."

He couldn't believe it. He stared at her for a moment in astonishment, then grabbed her in his arms and rolled until she was beneath him.

"You're sure?" he demanded. "You won't change your mind?"

She began to laugh. "I won't change my mind, darling. I love you too much for that."

Quinn felt like a helium-filled balloon, floating somewhere near the ceiling. He began to kiss her, feeling a surge of power that came with the knowledge that he wasn't going to have to leave her after all. Or if he did, she would be waiting for him when he returned.

His body was more than ready to join in the celebration, and he laughed out loud when she acknowledged his reaction by aligning her body with his. She was his. By God! She was his!

Sometime during the night, Jennifer stirred enough to pull the covers around them. Quinn slept peacefully on. She lay beside him, trying to get used to his new looks. He was so handsome and she loved him so much.

The past twelve months had been difficult for her. But he didn't ever have to know that. Having Paul walk in on them that morning had created an uproar in the organization. When she had gone back into Haida's home after seeing Quinn off, Paul had been waiting for her.

"Too bad none of us were told earlier that you managed to convince your captors to let you go," he said as soon as she walked into the room. "We've all been frantic."

He still wore his arm in a sling. She walked up and touched his hand, and he jerked away.

"I can imagine how you must have felt. I've had nightmares remembering you and Randy lying there in the dusty road and not being able to do anything about it. I'm glad you're all right."

"It's obvious that we needn't have worried about you."

His anger rocketed around the room. And she knew she was going to have to say something.

"It isn't what you think, Paul. I'm sorry if I've hurt you—"

"Hurt me! Hah! I'm just glad I found out this way. You've always been so standoffish with everyone. I was being so careful not to rush you in any way. That's a laugh, isn't it? Obviously you're the kind of woman who enjoys being brutalized and treated like a slut."

"Don't, Paul. Please don't. You and I are friends. Nothing has changed."

"Nothing has changed! My God, Jennifer. I find you sleeping with some Shiranese creep, one of the ones that almost killed us. Haida told me he had brought you here."

So Haida hadn't told anyone his true nationality. Bless her for that. "He was getting me back to Sirocco."

"For a big fat reward, of course."

"No."

"Well, I don't care. You can sleep with every terrorist in Shiran for all I care." He walked out of the room.

Unfortunately, he allowed his hurt to build so that within a few days after they returned to Sirocco, she realized that he had told everyone his interpretation of what he had seen.

If she had thought it would make any difference, she would have explained who Quinn was, but in doing so she might have jeopardized his position and endangered his life. She couldn't do that.

In the final analysis Jennifer realized that she could not control what other people thought about her, no matter what she said or what explanations she offered. It hurt, because these were people that she loved, that she had worked alongside for years.

They thought she had bought her freedom with her body, which was laughable, really. The Shiranese soldiers who had captured her would not have considered her body of any value and would have taken it, anyway.

Quinn stirred, reaching for her even in his slumber. She moved closer and allowed his warmth and love to lull her back to sleep. They were together now. That was all that mattered.

Quinn felt Jennifer stir beside him, and he tightened his hold on her. She kissed his chin and whispered, "I'll be back." He felt the bed shift and knew she was gone. He rolled over onto his stomach and stretched. He couldn't remember the last time he'd slept so well. If he wasn't feeling so lazy he'd look to see what time it was. From the light coming through his closed eyelids, he would guess it was morning.

He needed to call Max and tell him— Tell him what? Tell him he was in love and was getting married? He smiled to himself, imagining Max's reaction.

He heard Jennifer walk back into the room, then felt the bed move as she leaned against it.

"Quinn?"

"Hmm?" he responded, too content to open his eyes.

"I would like to introduce you to Angela, your daughter."

Epilogue

―――

Damn it, Jennifer, would you put that blasted thing down?''

"I thought you promised you wouldn't curse anymore in front of the children."

"My God, woman, you'd test the patience of a saint."

"And we all know that you're no saint, don't we?"

"Now don't start that."

Quinn and Jennifer stood outside a rather primitive hut on the outskirts of a small village high in the Andes Mountains in South America. They had just finished getting it ready for one of the women who had helped them in the Feed the Children program.

Jennifer brushed a few flying wisps of hair out of her eyes and looked around for five-year-old Angela. When she spotted the little girl, she smiled and touched Quinn's arm.

"Darling, look what your daughter is doing."

Quinn frowned, knowing that she was trying to change the subject. He glanced behind him and saw Angela sticking flowers in her three-year-old sister's hair. He grinned, thinking once again that it was hard to believe the two girls were sisters. Sheryl looked just like her mother, with fine blond hair and blue eyes. Although Angela's eyes were blue, they were dark, almost navy, and her hair was jet black.

He put his arms around Jennifer and pulled her close, loving the feel of her pressed against him. "You're changing the subject," he accused her.

"The table isn't heavy, Quinn," she replied in a soothing voice. "I just wanted to move it—"

"If you want something moved, ask me, okay?" He ran his hand over her slightly rounded abdomen.

She stroked his cheek, enjoying the feel of the silky beard that he'd only recently grown. "I would never do anything that might injure your son, love. Surely you know that."

Quinn lifted his brow. "My son? Have you been looking at your crystal ball lately?"

"Surely this time we'll have a boy."

He grinned. "That's what you said before Sheryl was born."

"Well, all we can do is keep trying, you know."

Quinn began to laugh at her resigned expression and hugged her to him once again.

"I've enjoyed this summer, haven't you?" she asked after a moment, enjoying the feel of his hands massaging her back.

"Very much."

"I know it's been a little primitive, living like this, but I think it's good for all of us to remember what it's like to get back to the basics."

"Do you, now? Were you afraid I'd forget?"

She turned in his arms so that she was leaning against his chest, looking out at the vista spread around them. "No. Maybe I'm the one who needs to be reminded once in a while, so I can truly appreciate all that I have."

"The girls have enjoyed it," he pointed out. "They've learned as much Spanish as we have and chatter in both languages with no problems." He nibbled on her neck and she shivered. "I have to admit that I'm looking forward to getting back home, though. I miss the hot tub and our large bed. I must be getting old."

"Not so you'd notice," she said, pressing her hips into him slightly.

"Behave," he said, nipping her earlobe.

Angela and Sheryl came trotting over to them.

"Look, Mama, see what I did to Sheryl?" Angela looked up at them proudly.

Sheryl patted her head and smiled.

Quinn felt that he was watching the scene as an observer, seeing the man with the beautiful wife snuggled in his arms, the two little girls standing there looking so healthy and content with their world.

And he wondered how had he gotten so lucky? How could he have known all those years ago when he walked into a small dusty room in a forgotten desert country that his destiny was waiting for him there?

He thought about the race across the desert, the horrendous dust storm, the last night they were together, then finding Jennifer in D.C. And he would never forget that fateful morning when Jennifer had brought Angela in to see him for the first time....

Jennifer's soft words had a galvanizing effect on Quinn. From being totally relaxed and more than half asleep, he jerked upright like a spring toy that had been overwound.

"My daughter!" he repeated in a strangled voice.

Jennifer was standing at the end of the bed, wearing a deep blue robe that emphasized the blue of her eyes. But for the moment, all of Quinn's attention was on the infant she was holding.

The baby was propped on one of Jennifer's arms, while Jennifer's other hand, spread against the baby's stomach, held her in position. Quinn stared at the small child whose blue eyes were so dark that they almost looked black, while Angela watched him with equal fascination.

"Here," Jennifer said casually and walked around the bed to where Quinn sat. She placed the infant in Quinn's arms and stepped back.

He stared down in dismay. He'd never been this close to such a little person before. She kicked her feet and he thought he would drop her. He brought her closer to his chest and one of her waving arms brushed against him and tiny fingers clasped a handful of chest hair.

Jennifer began to laugh when he flinched. She reached over and disentangled the tiny fingers. "Say hello to your daddy, sweetheart."

"My daughter," he repeated slowly, trying to overcome the shock. Short black curls clustered around her head and he hesitantly touched one. It felt so silky and fine. She wore a disposable diaper and a cotton shirt with little lambs embroidered on it. She made a gurgling sound and smiled, and dimples flashed in her cheeks.

He had a daughter. A real, live, kicking, armwaving, hair-pulling daughter. She was his. And he'd had no idea. None at all. He looked up at Jennifer and she was blurry. He blinked his eyes a couple of times and cleared his throat. "So much for the rhythm method of birth control," he managed to say, attempting a lightness he didn't feel.

He had helped to create this perfect little girl child. She had been created out of the awesome love he felt for Jennifer. She had been created out of his desire to show the woman he loved all the pleasure he could possibly share with her. And this was his reward.

He laid the baby on his shoulder and felt her tiny knees pull into him. Her head fit into the hollow of his neck as though made to size. Carefully he rubbed his hand across her tiny back, loving the powdery scent of her, the delicate weight of her.

His daughter.

Never before had he experienced such a sense of loving protectiveness. Here was a part of him, a part of who he was, what he was, what he hoped to become. Here was his future.

"I wish I'd known," he finally said, closing his eyes. He wanted to experience her in every way he could.

"There was no way I could let you know, Quinn," Jennifer said quietly, sitting down beside him. "Surely you must know that."

"I suppose my logic can accept that, but right at the moment my emotions aren't willing to." He forced himself to look at her. "I should have been there, you know. You needed me and I wasn't there for you."

She smiled. "Oh, but you were in many ways. I felt your presence with me. I felt your love, your tenderness. I knew that if there had been any way, you would have been there by my side, holding my hand, encouraging me."

Now that he thought about it, he realized that he had unconsciously registered the changes in her body the night before…the increased fullness of her breasts, a little more weight that added to her shapeliness.

"Why didn't you tell me last night?"

She shook her head. "I tried to think of a way, but I couldn't. I knew it would be a shock. I had to find the right way to tell you."

"Does your family know I'm her father?"

She chuckled. "No. Believe me, they're going to be so relieved."

"What do you mean?"

"Well, without going into all the details, the story that followed me back to the States was that my captors made full use of me while I was in captivity. Everyone has been too polite to inquire too closely about her father, for fear I'd admit that I had no idea which one he was."

He frowned. "Technically speaking, I suppose I *was* one of your captors."

"No, darling. You rescued me, remember?"

He glanced down at the baby cuddled in his arms. "Some rescue."

"I thought it was a fair trade. If I had to give you up, at least I had a part of you with me."

He slid his hand beneath Jennifer's chin and lifted until her gaze met his. "She's beautiful, love. Just like her mother."

"I had hoped she'd have your eyes, but so far they've stayed blue."

"Is she why you returned to the States?"

"Mostly, yes."

"So even if I couldn't talk you into finding safety, our daughter could."

"Yes. When I realized that I was pregnant, I was no longer willing to take any chances on the political climate of Shiran. I returned home, explained to my parents about the pregnancy and told them that I wanted to have the baby."

"They accepted that?"

"They had no choice. Mandy and I managed quite well. For the first few months, I continued to travel and give speeches, asking for contributions. After that, I came back here and waited, and dreamed."

"I always said you had a great deal of courage, Jennifer. Nothing you have ever done has made me change my mind."

She leaned over and kissed his cheek. "Loving your child was very easy for me."

"Having a child alone . . . facing all the people you knew...accepting society's label...none of that could have been easy for you."

"It was a learning time for me, that's true. I had to learn what was truly important to me. All my life I've wanted to do something to make a difference in the world. During this past year, I had to learn that first I had to make a difference in my own life. I had to deal with me and what made me who I was. I had to allow other people to have whatever opinion they wanted of me. When it came right down to it, none of their opinions were as important to me as having your child."

"Did you consider having an abortion, or having her adopted?"

She shook her head. "Never. I wanted her from the first hint that I might be pregnant. That has never changed."

"I love you so much, Jennifer. You've gone through so much because of me that I hurt just thinking about it. Here I've been trying to get an understanding of what it would be like to be a husband these past few hours, and now I discover I'm a father." His smile was rueful. "All of this is going to take some getting used to."

"Oh, I don't know. I doubt that you'll have much trouble adjusting to your adoring women folk."

Standing there on a hillside holding Jennifer in his arms and watching Angela and Sheryl, Quinn remembered Jennifer's remark from several years before. She had been right once again. It hadn't been difficult at all to be surrounded by love and warmth and laughter and sharing.

He smiled to himself, remembering Max's reaction.

"What do you mean, you're getting married and you have a three-month-old daughter!"

They were sitting in Max's office in a forgotten building in D.C.

Quinn reached into his wallet. "You wanna see a picture of her? She's the cutest thing you'll ever—"

"No, damn it. I do not need to look at baby pictures. Quinn McNamara, I want to know what's going on. You're one of my best agents. You've been able to ferret out information that no one else suspected. You've saved more than one situation with your quick thinking and lightning reflexes. And now all you can do is sit there with a fatuous smile on your face, cooing about babies and weddings!"

"And I owe it all to you, Max. How would you like to be my best man?"

"To me? What the hell is going on? Have you lost your mind?"

"Nope. Maybe I've found my sanity, or at least I'm looking in the right direction."

"How am I involved in this scenario, anyway?"

"You sent me to that party last night."

"Last night! You met a woman last night and intend to get married? Listen, Quinn, why don't you hold on just a moment. Give some thought to what you're doing. Let's face it. Maybe you've been keeping too rigorous a schedule. I'll admit I've pushed you hard on this Shiran situation." Max waved his hand in a benign gesture. "You want to take a few months off? Fine. Do that. Get whatever this is out of your system. But don't marry some good-looking dame just because she gave you some sob story about the man who left her all alone."

Quinn folded his arms and listened patiently. When Max had stopped talking for a few minutes, Quinn asked, "Are you through?"

"That depends," Max replied.

"I'm the man who left her all alone. I'm talking about Jennifer Sheridan."

Max sat up in his chair, a look of horror on his face. "You mean Senator Sheridan's daughter?"

Quinn nodded.

"The one who was captured last year by the— And then you—" He stared at him as though lost for words. "Why, you son-of-a— You sure as hell took advantage of the situation, didn't you?"

Quinn flushed, but didn't say anything.

"And you just found out last night that she had your baby. What did she do? Slap you with a paternity suit?"

"No."

"And you think you can make everything all right by marrying her, huh?"

"I'm marrying Jennifer because I love her and because I believe that she loves me. Angela is my bonus." He could not control the smile that broke free at the thought of the tiny baby.

"Dear Lord, here comes that silly grin again." He held out his hand. "All right, give me the damn pictures."

Quinn handed them across the desk and Max glanced at them. "Looks like a typical baby to me. Sure got a mess of curly hair, doesn't it?"

"She," Quinn corrected. "She's a beauty."

"If you say so," Max replied, handing him back the pictures. "Does that mean what I think it means?"

Quinn lifted his brow in inquiry.

"Somehow I don't think I'm going to be able to coax you into leaving this newly discovered domestic bliss, am I?"

Quinn straightened in his chair and leaned forward. Before he could say anything, Max shook his head and let out a disgusted sigh.

"I didn't think so." He looked at Quinn with irritation. "A damned family man. Of all the people I have working for me, Quinn McNamara, you would be the last one I would expect to do such a thing to me."

Quinn began to laugh. "You sound downright betrayed!" he finally managed to say.

"That's just about the way I feel," Max replied.

"So what do we do now?"

"Any suggestions?"

"I thought I might retire from the air force."

"Then what?"

"I might work with the Feed the Children program. I'm impressed with what a few people have been instrumental in doing. I had a firsthand view of what a difference it made in Shiran. These people truly care. They want to help others to help themselves."

"Spare me the rhetoric, McNamara. Will you be traveling overseas with them?"

"I don't know, yet. It's just something I'm looking at."

"Daddy." Sheryl interrupted Quinn's thoughts about another time, another place.

"Yes, sugar."

"I'm hungry."

He stepped away from Jennifer and picked up his daughter. "We can't have that now, can we?" He took Angela's hand. "Let's go find something to eat, want to?" Jennifer slid her arm around his waist, and they started back to town to join the others.

Good old Max. He always worked all the angles, Quinn thought to himself, remembering. He had accepted the fact that Quinn wanted out of the air force, but convinced him that with his background and talent he could still be useful to Max in his travels, just by keeping his eyes and ears open and reporting what he discovered.

And he agreed to be best man at the wedding.

Sheryl rested her head on his chest and settled into his arms. Quinn glanced down at her bright curls and smiled. He had made certain from the first moment he knew that Jennifer was pregnant with Sheryl that he missed nothing about the process of pregnancy and the delivery.

"Quinn, would you please stop following me around as though you think I'm incapable of walking across the floor without you?" Jennifer had finally said when she was about seven months pregnant. "You're driving me crazy with your hovering!"

They were living in the Virginia countryside by that time, in an area of rolling hills that calmed his soul with the never ending beauty of the various scenes from their windows. Quinn turned to one of the windows and gazed outside.

"I think it's trying to snow."

"You're changing the subject."

"I'm not hovering. Not really."

"What do you call it?"

He turned and grinned at her. He knew his grin was more than a little sheepish.

"I'm just concerned about you. That's all. Besides, I wasn't with you when you carried Angela. I want to make up for that."

Jennifer walked over to him and slid her arm around his waist, leaning her head against his shoulder. "I appreciate your concern, I really do, but, Quinn, don't you think you've overdone it a little?"

"What do you mean?"

"You've read every book you could find on pregnancies . . . and nutrition . . . and natural childbirth . . . and childcare. You've gone with me to every doctor appointment and cross-examined the doctor after each visit. I swear you could pass a medical examination on obstetrics without attending a single class. Not only that, but if our Lamaze teacher should forget to show up some time, I know you could teach the entire procedure without missing a beat."

He tilted her chin slightly with his finger, then leaned down and kissed her very gently. He would never take this woman for granted nor forget to be grateful that she was now an integral part of his life.

"I love you, Jennifer," he whispered.

She went up on her toes and kissed him with a loving warmth. "I love you, too, darling. I'm sorry I'm being so grouchy. But you must admit that we've gone from one extreme to the other. I went through my first pregnancy mostly on my own. Now I feel as though you don't intend to let me out of your sight."

"I suppose I'm trying to make up to you for all you had to go through last time. You refuse to discuss it with me, but I know it must have been rough for you."

"Deciding to become a single mother isn't the easiest thing in the world, I'll admit, but that's behind us now and we can't allow it to affect the rest of our lives."

He stroked her back and massaged the area in her lower back that seemed to carry the most stress of the weight. ''I have a hunch I would have been the same way if I'd been with you then. I'm sorry if you're feeling too restricted.''

"Oh, Quinn. You are so good with me, and with Angela, and I know the new arrival will love you as much as we do. How could he resist?''

"He?''

"Surely this one will be a boy.''

He had been in the delivery room when Sheryl had arrived, announcing her annoyance to anyone who would listen. He would never forget the experience, and the sense of bonding that took place when the nurse had placed her in his arms. She had stopped crying and was blinking her eyes as though trying to focus on the brand-new world around her.

Just thinking about that moment three years later caused him to hug her closer to him. It had been an experience like none other, indescribable and unforgettable. He'd been unaware of the tears flowing down his cheeks until the nurse had leaned over and touched his shoulder, holding out a handkerchief with an understanding smile on her face.

It had been another moment in his life when the love he felt seemed to overflow from within him. Jennifer's arrival in his life had triggered off many such instances, and he had a hunch that he would experience that overwhelming sense of love and well-being often in the future. However, he knew that he would never take it for granted.

One of the native women met them at the entrance of the small hostel where they were staying, greeting Angela with hugs and chatter. Sheryl wiggled out of Quinn's arms and ran inside, pointing to her hair, which was laced with flowers, and talking as fast as she could. Quinn and Jennifer remained on the veranda.

"I think it's going to rain," Jennifer said, watching the distant mountains disappear behind cloud cover.

"What else is new?" Quinn said, draping his arm around her shoulder.

"I'm still going to miss this place," she said, leaning her head against his chest. "It's been so interesting here, getting to know the people, learning to understand their culture, their pride. And the family units are so strong."

"Yes. They've been quite an example for all of us."

She went up on tiptoe, kissing him. "We've got a fairly strong family unit, too, you know."

He nodded. "And I never take it for granted, because I know what a lost feeling it is not to have anyone to love, or to be loved by. To me that would truly be hell, to return to that existence."

"Well, if this one is another girl, you're going to have your own little harem of women at your beck and call."

"It doesn't matter what the baby is. I want all of them to understand love. To understand its power, to understand what a difference it can make in a life and how it can create peace wherever it goes."

The rain moved toward them and they watched, fascinated to see it advance with such grandeur.

The native woman stuck her head out the door and said she was putting the children down for their afternoon naps. They thanked her, then continued to watch as the wind picked up slightly, bringing with it the hint of fresh rain, the smell of green growing things, of life.

"Is it time for your nap?" Jennifer whispered.

Quinn looked down at the woman standing beside him and saw the love shining in her eyes. The sudden rush of feeling that swept over him at such times enveloped him and made him tremble. Without a word, he picked her up and carried her inside to spend a rainy afternoon in bed with the woman he loved.

*   *   *   *   *

Coming in July from

Silhouette Desire®

ODD MAN OUT #505
by Lass Small

Roberta Lambert is too busy with her job to notice that her new apartment-mate is a strong, desirable man. But Graham Rawlins has ways of getting her undivided attention....

Roberta is one of five fascinating Lambert sisters. She is as enticing as each one of her three sisters, whose stories you have already enjoyed or will want to read:

- Hillary in GOLDILOCKS AND THE BEHR (Desire #437)
- Tate in HIDE AND SEEK (Desire #453)
- Georgina in RED ROVER (Desire #491)

Watch for Book IV of Lass Small's terrific miniseries and read Fredricka's story in TAGGED (Desire #528) coming in October.

"GIVE YOUR HEART TO SILHOUETTE" SWEEPSTAKES
OFFICIAL RULES
NO PURCHASE NECESSARY TO ENTER OR RECEIVE A PRIZE

1. To enter and join the Silhouette Reader Service, rub off the concealment device on all game tickets. This will reveal the potential value for each Sweepstakes entry number and the number of free book(s) you will receive. Accepting the free book(s) will automatically entitle you to also receive a free bonus gift. If you do not wish to take advantage of our introduction to the Silhouette Reader Service but wish to enter the Sweepstakes only, rub off the concealment device on tickets #1-3 only. To enter, return your entire sheet of tickets. Incomplete and/or inaccurate entries are not eligible for that section or section (s) of prizes. Not responsible for mutilated or unreadable entries or inadvertent printing errors. Mechanically reproduced entries are null and void.

2. Either way, your Sweepstakes numbers will be compared against the list of winning numbers generated at random by computer. In the event that all prizes are not claimed, random drawings will be made from all entries received from all presentations to award all unclaimed prizes. All cash prizes are payable in U.S. funds. This is in addition to any free, surprise or mystery gifts that might be offered. The following prizes are awarded in this sweepstakes:

(1)	*Grand Prize	$1,000,000	Annuity
(1)	First Prize	$35,000	
(1)	Second Prize	$10,000	
(3)	Third Prize	$5,000	
(10)	Fourth Prize	$1,000	
(25)	Fifth Prize	$500	
(5000)	Sixth Prize	$5	

*The Grand Prize is payable through a $1,000,000 annuity. Winner may elect to receive $25,000 a year for 40 years, totaling up to $1,000,000 without interest, or $350,000 in one cash payment. Winners selected will receive the prizes offered in the Sweepstakes promotion they receive.

Entrants may cancel the Reader Service privileges at any time without cost or obligation to buy (see details in center insert card).

3. Versions of this Sweepstakes with different graphics may be offered in other mailings or at retail outlets by Torstar Corp. and its affiliates. This promotion is being conducted under the supervision of Marden-Kane, Inc., an independent judging organization. By entering this Sweepstakes, each entrant accepts and agrees to be bound by these rules and the decisions of the judges, which shall be final and binding. Odds of winning are dependent upon the total number of entries received. Taxes, if any, are the sole responsibility of the winners. Prizes are nontransferable. All entries must be received by March 31, 1990. The drawing will take place on April 30, 1990, at the offices of Marden-Kane, Inc., Lake Success, N.Y.

4. This offer is open to residents of the U.S., Great Britain and Canada, 18 years or older, except employees of Torstar Corp., its affiliates, and subsidiaries, Marden-Kane, Inc. and all other agencies and persons connected with conducting this Sweepstakes. All federal, state and local laws apply. Void wherever prohibited or restricted by law.

5. Winners will be notified by mail and may be required to execute an affidavit of eligibility and release that must be returned within 14 days after notification. Canadian winners will be required to answer a skill-testing question. Winners consent to the use of their name, photograph and/or likeness for advertising and publicity in conjunction with this and similar promotions without additional compensation. One prize per family or household.

6. For a list of our most current major prizewinners, send a stamped, self-addressed envelope to: WINNERS LIST, c/o MARDEN-KANE, INC., P.O. BOX 701, SAYREVILLE, N.J. 08871

If Sweepstakes entry form is missing, please print your name and address on a 3" × 5" piece of plain paper and send to:

In the U.S.	In Canada
Sweepstakes Entry	Sweepstakes Entry
901 Fuhrmann Blvd.	P.O. Box 609
P.O. Box 1867	Fort Erie, Ontario
Buffalo, NY 14269-1867	L2A 5X3

LTY-S69R

Silhouette Intimate Moments

COMING NEXT MONTH!

LIEUTENANT GABRIEL RODRIGUEZ
in
Something of Heaven

From his first appearance in Marilyn Pappano's popular *Guilt by Association*, Lieutenant Gabriel Rodriguez captured readers' hearts. Your letters poured in, asking to see this dynamic man reappear—this time as the hero of his own book. Next month, all your wishes come true in *Something of Heaven* (IM #294), Marilyn Pappano's latest romantic tour de force.

Gabriel longs to win back the love of Rachel Martinez, who once filled his arms and brought beauty to his lonely nights. Then he drove her away, unable to face the power of his feelings and the cruelty of fate. That same fate has given him a second chance with Rachel, but to take advantage of it, he will have to trust her with his darkest secret: somewhere in the world, Gabriel may have a son. Long before he knew Rachel, there was another woman, a woman who repaid his love with lies—and ran away to bear their child alone. Rachel is the only one who can find that child for him, but if he asks her, will he lose her love forever or, together, will they find *Something of Heaven*?

Next month only, read *Something of Heaven* and follow Gabriel on the road to happiness.

Silhouette Intimate Moments
Where the Romance Never Ends

IM294-1

Silhouette Desire ®

COMING NEXT MONTH

#505 ODD MAN OUT—Lass Small
July's *Man of the Month*, Graham Rawlins, was undeniably attractive, but Roberta Lambert seemed uninterested. However, Graham was very determined, and she found he'd do almost *anything* to get her attention....

#506 THE PIRATE O'KEEFE—Helen R. Myers
Doctor Laura Connell was intrigued by the injured man washed up on her beach. When she discovered his true identity it was too late—she'd fallen for the pirate O'Keefe.

#507 A WILDER NAME—Laura Leone
Luke Swain was positively the most irritating man Nina Gnagnarelli had ever met. He'd insulted her wardrobe, her integrity and her manners. He'd also set her heart on fire!

#508 BLIND JUSTICE—Cathryn Clare
As far as Lily Martineau was concerned, successful corporate lawyer Matt Malone was already married—to his job. Matt pleaded guilty as charged, then demanded a retrial.

#509 ETERNALLY EVE—Ashley Summers
Nate Wright had left Eve Sheridan with a broken heart. Now he seemed to have no memory of her—but it was a night Eve would never forget!

#510 MAGIC TOUCH—Noelle Berry McCue
One magic night with a handsome stranger made Caroline Barclay feel irresistible. But she didn't believe in fairy tales until James Mitchel walked back into her life—as her new boss.

AVAILABLE NOW:

Silhouette Special Edition

presents

★ LOVE AND GLORY ★

from
Lindsay McKenna

Introducing a gripping new series celebrating our men—and women—in uniform. Meet the Trayherns, a military family as proud and colorful as the American flag, a family fighting the shadow of dishonor, a family determined to triumph—with
LOVE AND GLORY!

June: A QUESTION OF HONOR (SE #529) leads the fast-paced excitement. When Coast Guard officer Noah Trayhern offers Kit Anderson a safe house, he unwittingly endangers his own guarded emotions.

July: NO SURRENDER (SE #535) Navy pilot Alyssa Trayhern's assignment with arrogant jet jockey Clay Cantrell threatens her career—and her heart—with a crash landing!

August: RETURN OF A HERO (SE #541) Strike up the band to welcome home a man whose top-secret reappearance will make headline news . . . with a delicate, daring woman by his side.